The Mystery at Greystone Hall

Books by Norah Smaridge

The Mystery at Greystone Hall
The Secret of the Brownstone House

The Mystery at Greystone Hall

NORAH SMARIDGE

Illustrated by Robert Handville

DODD, MEAD & COMPANY

NEW YORK

1 2 3 4 5 6 7 8 9 10

Library of Congress Cataloging in Publication Data

Smaridge, Norah.
The mystery at Greystone Hall.

SUMMARY: While vacationing in England, a young sleuth
becomes involved in a mystery at Greystone Hall.
[1. Mystery and detective stories. 2. England—
Fiction] I. Handville, Robert. II. Title.
PZ7.S6392My [Fic] 79-52045
ISBN 0-396-07733-1

For my young friend and neighbor,
KIM LANGE

1

Robin Miller had been thinking hard and getting nowhere. Now she sighed and looked at her mother. "I'll settle for Camp Fatso," she said. "If that's okay with you and Daddy."

"Camp Fatso?"

Her mother's eyebrows shot up, and Robin laughed. "That's not its real name," she said. "It's what Bunny and Eve call it." Bunny and Eve were her best friends. They were both rather fat, but they were fun and bright and she loved them. "It's a camp for fat girls."

"But you're *not* fat," her mother said crossly. "You have a lovely figure."

"There's too much of it. I'd like my bones to show," Robin said. "At Camp Fatso they make you ride in the hills at dawn. And dive into icy lakes—to get the pounds off you." Her mother didn't even smile, so Robin went on, "Okay, if not Camp Fatso, then what?"

She didn't really expect an answer. Mom and

7

Daddy had run out of ideas for what their darling daughter could do this summer. Stay with Aunt Rose (two little kids, sweet but sticky). Go to music camp (she wasn't all that musical). Take summer courses (ugh).

The trouble was that nothing looked exciting after last summer. That had been really wild. Staying in New York City, catching a kidnapper—or rather a monkeynapper. . . .

The mailman whistled and Robin made for the door. There might be something for her. She rather hoped not. Getting letters was nice, but you had to answer them.

There was nothing for Robin. Only a letter for her mother in Aunt Val's splashy handwriting. Aunt Val, Daddy's sister, was a buyer of paintings in New York City. She took trips all over the world.

The letter was a long one. Robin watched her mother's face as she read. It was slowly going pink. Something is getting Mom excited, Robin thought. She looks so sweet when she's excited. Like a little kid.

Her mother finished reading and smiled at Robin. "Here's your summer, and you're in luck again! Aunt Val wants to take you with her to England!"

Robin stared. England! No wonder Mom had gone pink. "But—but that's three thousand miles away," she said, her voice a squeak. "Daddy would never let me go so far!"

"He'll trust you with Aunt Val," her mother said. "We'll talk it over when he gets home, and I'll give her a call tonight."

Her mother was right. Her father was willing to let Robin go with his sister. "You'll be safe with Val," he said. "And you're not likely to have another crazy time like last summer." He put an arm around her and hugged her. "About the worst you could do is get yourself locked up in the Tower of London after hours."

"Good idea," Robin said. "Think of the ghosts I'd meet."

It was almost eleven before her mother caught up with Aunt Val on the telephone. Robin, on her way to bed, passed her parents' room and looked in. Her mother was telling Aunt Val how delighted they all were.

Then Robin stiffened as her mother's voice changed. "But Val, dear," she said, "you won't want Robin glued to you every minute. What will you do with her when you have a date? You can't let her run loose in a city as big as London!"

Robin couldn't hear Aunt Val's answer. But it must have been satisfactory. Mom was making those little cooing sounds she made when she was pleased. Suddenly Robin forgot about honor and edged closer so that she could hear.

"You'll get her an escort from an escort service?" her mother cried, "Oh, Val, how clever of you. They can take her to all the places you've seen a dozen times!" She laughed. "Though I'm sure Robin will have her own ideas—like asking to meet Prince Charles."

Robin frowned. Now Mother was being silly. But the escort service sounded like fun. She wondered if Mom knew that there were escort services in New York City. You read about them in magazines like *Cue.* She and Bunny and Eve often looked at the men's pictures and picked out the one they'd most like to be escorted by. Her own choice was Bill Barber. Of course he was a bit old looking, twenty-four at least. But if she remembered not to squeak when she was surprised, she could easily pass for seventeen.

She went to do her face for the night. Thank goodness she had a clear skin, not like poor Eve who was very pretty but always breaking out.

Robin wondered if the escort would take her anywhere at night. Aunt Val would surely have some evening dates. Maybe the escort would take Robin to the theatre. Or to a London disco. She was a good dancer.

She was passing her parents' room again when she heard her father's voice. He sounded very wide awake. "Escort service?" he said, "Oh, no, I don't think I could go along with that. They'd drag the poor girl into old churches, and you know Robin. The minute she had enough, she'd give them the slip."

"Oh, Bill, don't be like that!" her mother said. "Robin could tell them what she wanted to see. And I'm sure anyone Val hired could be trusted to keep a careful eye on her. After all, Robin doesn't really go looking for trouble."

"It just comes to her," her father said. "I'll have to give the matter some thought."

Robin crept past her parents' door and went to her own room. "Oh, Daddy," she sighed. "Why do you have to *worry* about me so?"

2

Ten days later, Robin and her aunt were at Kennedy Airport, boarding Flight 72 for London. "Where have they gone with our cases?" Robin asked, frowning. "Eve's mother lost all her stuff when she flew to Paris." How terrible if they landed in London with only the clothes they stood up in! She thought unhappily of her two new suits (two, because the English lived in suits when they were not living in raincoats).

Aunt Val made light of her fears. "I've never lost so much as a bobby pin," she said. She glanced quickly around the cabin. "No one very exciting looking," she whispered.

"I'll take a closer look," Robin said. "Exciting people don't always *look* exciting." She walked the length of the plane, as if she were looking for a friend.

But the passengers seemed a dull lot. Two women with their noses already in books. Some businessmen with bald heads. A mother with two little kids. "There's no one who looks at all like a hijacker," she told Aunt Val, squeezing past her to the window seat. "Too bad. It would be fun if someone ordered the plane to some dark jungle."

"You think so?" Aunt Val said mildly. She was used to Robin's flights of fancy.

Robin nodded. "Even if we ended up in a cannibal's cooking pot." Aunt Val didn't seem to care for that idea, so she added kindly, "I'd get us out somehow."

"I believe you," Aunt Val said. She made herself comfortable. "I don't know about you, Robin, but I can use a nap."

Robin was wide awake. She decided to look through the papers in the pocket on the back of the seat in front of her. Maps. Folders. Post-cards of the plane in a bright blue sky.

She wrote two wish-you-were-here's to Bunny and Eve. They'd be at Camp Fatso by now. Running a mile before breakfast—and then gobbling a mountain of pancakes with butter and honey.

After a while she closed her eyes and gave

herself up to her latest dream. A dream about the young man from the escort service. He'd be tall and dark, with perhaps a beard, or a little moustache.

She hadn't said anything to Aunt Val about the escort service. For one thing, she wasn't supposed to know about it. For another, Aunt Val might think she was planning some sort of caper. She was as bad as Mom and Daddy that way.

Robin hadn't anything in mind, really. She only meant to let him take her to something lively. Like the London Zoo. And she wanted to visit Scotland Yard, where the famous English detectives hung out.

Hours later, after meals and snacks and more naps, Aunt Val shook Robin by the arm. "Wake up, dear! We're here."

Robin rubbed her eyes. "In England?" She looked out the window—nothing but darkness and a few lights peppering the airfield. "I was dreaming we were on a beach in Pago Pago, wherever that is." She got her things together and followed Aunt Val off the plane, telling the flight attendant a polite goodbye.

A small bus took them across the huge airfield to the terminal and they made their way to the customs. Aunt Val was right. Robin's suitcases were waiting for her. The customs man didn't even make her open them. He just made marks on them and said, "Enjoy your stay with us."

"There's an airport bus to the city but it crawls," Aunt Val said, "We'll take a cab."

It was two o'clock in the morning by English time, and a dark, moonless night. "No peasoup fog," Robin said. "In those tales about Jack the Ripper—the one who knifed all the girls—there's always a peasoup fog."

Aunt Val smiled. "I think that's a thing of the past, like the Ripper himself."

Looking through the window, Robin could make out little in the shadowy streets. She was almost asleep again when the cab pulled up at the Hotel Parkside.

The owner-manager came down the steps to meet them. "How nice to have you with us again, Miss Miller," he said, shaking hands with Aunt Val. "And you're lucky in the weather this time."

"My niece was expecting a peasoup fog," Aunt Val told him, smiling and shaking hands. "Robin, this is Mr. Roper."

Mr. Roper smiled at Robin. "I'm happy to meet one of America's long-stemmed beauties," he said. "Isn't that what they call your good-looking girls?"

Robin's smile thanked him for the pretty speech, but sleepily. "Robin's dead on her feet," Aunt Val said. "She only catnapped all the way over. Why not go on up to your room, dear? I want to talk to Mr. Roper for a few minutes, and read my mail."

"Your room is Number 6, at the head of the stairs," Mr. Roper said. "The bellboy will show you." He looked around but there was no sign of the bellboy, and he shook his head. "Looks as if he's gone into hiding." He didn't seem cross about it.

"I'll find my way," Robin said.

17

The door of Number 6 was partly open, and the bedside lamp was turned on. Robin went in, pulled off her coat, and tossed it on the bed.

Cold air blew through the two windows. Moving to lower them, she stopped suddenly. Near a window was a small armchair. And in it, fast asleep, was the missing bellboy.

3

Robin came closer and stood looking down at the boy. Fast asleep, poor guy. And no wonder. It was nearly 3:00 A.M. Most likely he had stayed up just to carry their cases.

He was very nice looking, Robin thought. Thick, fair hair, a straight nose, and skin as clear as a baby's. Not like some of the boys at school, who were good looking but had bumps and things.

She'd better wake him up—but how? If she gave him a poke, he might yell. Robin frowned. How did you get sleeping English boys to their feet?

She had an idea. He would surely spring to attention for "God Save the Queen." She could try singing it close to his ear. She knew some of the words, and the tune was the same as "My Country, 'Tis of Thee."

Bending down until her lips almost touched

his ear, she began to sing softly. She got as far as "Send her victorious" when the boy's eyes flew open. He stared up at Robin and got to his feet.

"Hi, there," Robin said, pleased with herself. "I thought that would do the trick."

The boy looked at her, reddening. "Terribly sorry, madam," he said. "I just wanted to see what it felt like to sit down. I haven't sat down for a week." He added, "Madam."

"Poor you," Robin said in her softest voice. "But please stop calling me 'madam.' I'm not all that old." She held out her hand. "My name's Robin Miller and I'm an American."

"So I hear. I like the way you talk," the boy said. "I'm Mark Roper—and I'd better get your bags before the manager comes roaring for me."

He was back in a minute, carrying Robin's cases as if they were feather light. "Would you like me to pull down the shades?" he asked.

Robin followed him to the window and

looked across the street at treetops. "Is that really a park down there?" she asked.

"A pocket-sized one. We call them 'squares,' and London's got a lot of them. Nice for old ladies, and dogs," Mark said. Robin liked his voice. It was clipped and clear and went up and down in a different way from American voices.

"Tell me what to see in London," Robin said. She was wide awake now and wanted to hear him talk some more. "Not churches or old buildings, though. I like spooky places. Like where Jack the Ripper bumped off all those young women."

"Jack the Ripper?" Mark looked surprised. "Isn't he a bit old hat by now?" He looked at Robin consideringly. "If you're really out for blood you should head for Madame Tussaud's."

"Never heard of her," Robin said truthfully.

He looked as if this were hard to believe. Then he straightened up and, smiling, began to recite:

"There was an old woman named Tussaud
Who loved the grand folk of *Who's Who* so
That she made them in wax
Both their fronts and their backs
And asked no permission to do so."

"Nice," Robin said. "But I'm not much wiser—and there's nothing about blood."

Mark's eyebrows rose. "Madame Tussaud's is the biggest and best wax museum in the world. It's got everything—figures from history, art, space. Everyone from King Henry VII to Muhammad Ali. But what *you'll* fall for is the Chamber of Horrors. It has life-size figures of murderers—caught in the act!"

"Like who?" Robin asked.

"Jack the Ripper, for one. And Crippen. He murdered his wife because she thought she could sing. And there's Mrs. Dyer. She did in forty-six of the babies left in her care and tossed their bodies into the river."

Robin squeaked. "Oh, don't. I like babies."

Mark laughed. "You asked for it, didn't you?"

22

Robin was about to answer when Aunt Val appeared in the doorway. "I thought you'd be asleep long ago, Robin," she said. Out of the corner of her eye, Robin saw Mark leave, and Aunt Val staring after him. "I see you're already getting on with the English," she said.

"I had to be polite," Robin said. "We kept him up so late."

Aunt Val sat on the edge of the bed. "He looks like a nice boy. And he's not really a bellboy. Mr. Roper is his uncle, and this boy came to help while the real bellboy is sick."

"I don't care *what* he is," Robin said, starting to undress. Grownups were so silly, she thought. Always bothering about what people *were.* "I like him. He's been telling me what to see in London." She wondered if Aunt Val would go with her to Madame Tussaud's. Not into the Chamber of Horrors, anyway. Aunt Val was one of those women who scream at mice and spiders.

"About sightseeing," Aunt Val said, looking upset. "I had hoped to have a few days when

23

I could show you around. But now I find I have to go to Cornwall to bid for a painting—and I can't take you with me."

Robin smiled at her. "That's okay," she said kindly. "I can always hop a bus and go places."

"Oh, no—no," Aunt Val said. "I'm afraid that's out. I promised your father not to let you loose in London." She got up to leave. "But I think things will work out all right. Mr. Roper told me of a very good escort service. I'll call them in the morning and ask them to send someone to take you around."

4

Next morning Robin woke slowly, wondering where she was. She looked at the folding clock on the bedside table. Twenty past eleven!

Then she remembered. She was in London, at the Hotel Parkside. Aunt Val had told her to sleep as long as she liked.

She remembered something else, something that made her wide awake. The last thing Aunt Val had talked about was the escort service. In a little while she, Robin Miller, would be meeting the young man who would take her around London, starting—Robin smiled—with Madame Tussaud's Chamber of Horrors.

Jumping out of bed, she took a quick shower and put on the nicer of her two suits. Rust color, with a swingy skirt that would spin around to show her nice legs. Daddy always said she had good legs, even better than Mom's.

Late though it was, the Hotel Parkside was

still serving breakfast. Robin followed her nose downstairs and along the hall to the dining room. There was a wonderful smell of bacon and eggs and—what was it?—sausage?

Aunt Val was already at table, sipping her coffee as if it were medicine. "Don't take the coffee," she whispered. "I think it's made with cabbage water." Aloud she said, "How do you do it? Up most of the night, yet here you are, bright-eyed and bushy-tailed."

"And so hungry I could eat a horse," Robin said.

Aunt Val shook her head. "The English would take a dim view of that. They're great animal lovers. You'd better settle for bacon and eggs."

"And sausage," Robin said. Looking round the sunny room, she saw Mark Roper, carrying a tray. So he waited tables as well as being a bellboy. She hoped he would see her stepping out with the escort.

Aunt Val took an envelope out of her bag

and handed it to Robin. "English money. You'll soon get the hang of it."

Robin gave the notes a quick look. "I won't have to worry my head about it, will I?" she said. "I mean, the escort will do all the paying, won't he?"

Aunt Val started. Her eyebrows rose. "*He*?" she said. She laughed nervously. "Robin, you don't imagine that the escort will be a *man*?"

"Of course he will," Robin said, surprised. "I've seen ads in *Cue* for escort services. They have male escorts for the women and women escorts for the men." She wondered why Aunt Val looked so taken aback. "Bunny and I sometimes pretend to pick the one we'd like to be escorted by. She always chooses a father figure. As for Eve—"

She stopped. Mark Roper was coming to their table with a tray. "Good morning, ladies," he said. He set down a fat brown teapot. "Another beautiful day, the kind we order for Americans."

It was a good thing that Aunt Val had opened the *London Mail.* Because she didn't see Robin lift the teapot—and find a small, folded note under it. Pleasantly surprised, Robin opened the note on her lap. Aunt Val, luckily, was deep in the news.

Robin read: "I'll look out for you in the Chamber of Horrors this afternoon about three."

Robin looked across the room and saw Mark. She gave a little wave. Nice that Mark, too, was going to Madam Tussaud's. Even if she was with an escort, she could stop and talk for a while.

She suddenly noticed that Aunt Val had dropped her newspaper and was staring across the room. "Oh, no—no," Aunt Val said, under her breath.

What was she in such a state about? Robin's glance followed her aunt's and she, too, started. A funny-looking little lady was making her way between the tables. "She's like Mary Poppins," Robin thought. "She's even wearing

28

a hat." Back home, nobody wore hats, except to go to church.

And she was carrying an umbrella big enough to fly on!

Suddenly the little woman spotted Aunt Val and made for their table. "You must be Miss Miller, from Boston, U.S.A.," she said. She had a high, sweet voice, Robin noticed, and a nice but shaky smile. "How nice to meet you. I'm Emma Tilly—from the escort service."

5

From the escort service. Robin stared at Emma Tilly, not believing her eyes. She glanced quickly at her aunt, but Aunt Val would not meet her look.

The little woman turned to Robin. "You must be the young lady I'm going to take under my wing," she said. Robin noticed that her voice shook a little.

Why, she's scared of me, Robin thought. No wonder. Both of us staring at the poor little lady as if she had just landed from outer space.

Suddenly Robin remembered Betsy Wells, the new girl who had joined their class last term. Miss Brown, their teacher, had presented her to the class, and Betsy had stood in front of them, red in the face. Not a pretty girl. Limp hair. Wires on her teeth.

Robin had been sorry for her. "Nice to have you with us, Betsy," she had said, shaking the girl's cold hand. "After class I'll show you

31

around, if you like."

Miss Brown had been pleased with Robin, but Robin wondered why. Surely no one liked to see another person looking so unhappy, like a fish out of water? You had to do *something* to make them feel at home.

And this little woman looked almost as scared as Betsy Wells. Robin would just have to make her feel welcome. "Nice to have you, Miss Tilly," Robin said, with her warmest smile. "If I looked—well, surprised—it's only because I was sort of expecting a *man.* How silly can I get?" She turned to Aunt Val. "They wouldn't send a man to take out a girl as young as I am. I keep forgetting I'm not seventeen. Or even sixteen."

Miss Tilly returned Robin's smile. "I often wish I were a man," she said. "It would be much easier to get taxis. Even a *short* man can get a taxi easier than a woman can." She looked at Aunt Val. "But I'm a good escort. I've been at it for years."

Aunt Val smiled as warmly as Robin had

32

done. "We're lucky to get you, Miss Tilly. I wish I didn't have to rush away." She turned to Robin. "Darling, have a wonderful afternoon. Have tea somewhere—the English are very good at teas—and we'll have dinner together when I get back."

Robin smiled to herself. Aunt Val only called her "darling" when she was extra pleased with her. She must have thought Robin was going to kick up a fuss. Refuse to go with Miss Tilly, maybe? As if she could be so mean. True, Miss Tilly looked a little—well, out-of-the-way—but she had a nice smile and a sweet, friendly voice.

Taking charge, Robin ordered fresh tea for Miss Tilly. "And have some raisin toast. The raisins are a bit hard but it tastes good." She hoped Miss Tilly wouldn't chip a tooth on it. She had good white teeth, but they poked a bit.

Miss Tilly, Robin thought, should be easier to handle than a male escort. She decided to try her out. "Miss Tilly, could we go to the

33

wax museum this afternoon? To Madame Somebody's."

Miss Tilly beamed. "Madame Tussaud's? Why, of course we can. It's one of my favorite places. Most Americans ask to be taken to Westminster Abbey and St. Paul's Cathedral—and I get so tired of them. All those gravestones. So depressing!" She looked at Robin thoughtfully. "But I'd better warn you that you *do* need a strong stomach for the Chamber of Horrors."

Robin laughed. "I guess mine's strong enough. At home I'm the one who has to pick up the poor little dead mice our cat brings in. He lays them at Mom's feet and she screams the place down!"

Some hours later, after doing some sightseeing, they climbed to the top deck of one of London's red buses. "Shall I point things out?" Miss Tilly asked. "Or shall we just talk?"

"Just talk," Robin said. "By the time you pointed, we'd be past whatever it is." She added, "Tell me about Madame Tussaud. Running a wax museum seems a funny job for a woman. Even today, when women climb telephone poles and dig coal."

"Oh, Madame was far ahead of her time," Miss Tilly said. "She was a Swiss girl, Marie Gresholtz, born in 1761, but she lived in France. All her people except one uncle were killed during the French Revolution, so she lived with her uncle. He taught her how to make beeswax models."

"Not very useful," Robin said.

"Oh, but it was! Because when Marie was thrown into prison for being a Republican, her modeling saved her life. Her jailers set her to making masks of all the prisoners who had their heads chopped off!"

"You mean she made them from the dead bodies?" Robin's voice was a squeak.

"Just the heads," Miss Tilly told her. "They used to bring them to her on a tray—while they were still fresh."

"And dripping with blood," Robin said. "Ugh." Miss Tilly, she thought, was going to

35

be far more fun than a male escort. A man would never tell a young girl hair-raising stories. Daddy didn't even like her watching murder stuff on TV.

"They set Marie free at last and she came to England," Miss Tilly went on. "She went all around the country with a waxwork show. And after a time she came to London, and the show just grew and grew—" she stopped. "Oh, here we are, Robin." She pointed down the block. "See that building with the flags?"

Robin murmured something. She really wasn't listening any more. Halfway down the block was a familiar figure. Though he looked a little different without his bellboy uniform.

6

"Is something the matter?" Miss Tilly asked as Robin stared down the street.

"Oh, no," Robin said. "I thought I saw Mark Roper heading for Madame Tussaud's. He's the bellboy at the hotel."

"I know. I know Mark very well," Miss Tilly said. "He always spends part of the summer with his uncle. When he was younger he used often to come along when I had young people from the hotel to take around." She added, "He's a very nice boy, Mark."

"I think so too," Robin said. It was good that Miss Tilly knew Mark—and liked him. It would make it easier for her to stop and talk to him. They might even invite him to tea! "We talked a bit last night when he carried up my cases. As a matter of fact, it was Mark who told me not to miss Madame Tussaud's."

They reached the entrance and bought their tickets. There was a crowd going in and buses lined up outside, unloading dozens of visitors. Most had cameras over their shoulders.

"Let's just step into the Grand Hall for a minute to make our bows to Madame Tussaud," Miss Tilly said. "She's one figure you really mustn't miss."

The Grand Hall was well named, Robin thought. It was a huge room, lined with wax figures that stretched as far as the eye could see. It would take days to look at everything properly, she thought. No wonder Mark came here so often.

"You can stare as much as you like, but make sure you're not staring at a real live person," Miss Tilly said. "A lady poked me with her umbrella once—quite sharply! I thought she was wax and I went up close to look at her nose. It was such a funny shape."

Robin laughed, trying to squeeze her way through the people who were pushing to look at Madame Tussaud. When she at last wiggled to the front, she looked curiously at the seated figure. It was somehow scary. She ought to be in the Chamber of Horrors herself, Robin thought. She has a cruel face.

Madame looked like somebody's great-great-great grandmother. Maybe older. She wore a white bonnet, black-rimmed glasses, and a long black satin dress with a high neck. Her black eyes stared coldly ahead, her lips were thin and tightly closed. "That's enough of *her*," Robin said, turning around to Miss Tilly.

Miss Tilly sensed that Robin was eager to get to the Chamber of Horrors. "We'll take the lift," she said. "The Chamber is sunk way below ground level."

They were the only people in the elevator. It jerked slowly on its way down, down, down. "To the bowels of the earth," Robin said. She smiled. "I've always wanted a chance to say that."

They got out of the elevator and she looked ahead of them, satisfied. The outside of the Chamber of Horrors was dark and grim. "It's modeled after that terrible French prison, La

Force," Miss Tilly whispered. And added, "Why do I always whisper down here!"

Robin waited a minute. "Abandon hope, all ye who enter here!" she said. But she stepped forward hopefully enough. At first she could hardly see. The lights were dim—to make it creepy, she supposed.

Suddenly she jumped. She was staring at a homely looking bathtub. It seemed harmless, until she noticed the man sliding down in it. His face was white and blood was spilling from his chest.

"That's Marat, the French revolutionary," Miss Tilly said in a low voice. "He had some skin trouble and he had to take warm baths for it. He used to sit in the tub, writing in his notebook. One day a young woman got into his house. She said she had news for him—and she ran into the bathroom and stabbed him in the heart!"

"Wow," Robin said, turning away. "It would have been safer for him to take showers!"

Miss Tilly laughed nervously and they moved

slowly along. "We seem to be the only visitors," Miss Tilly said. "I suppose everyone is looking at the new figures—tennis stars, mostly."

It's not a place you could forget easily, Robin thought, stopping to look at a figure of a kindly looking man with glasses and a moustache. All these faces, alike and yet not alike. Great spooky dolls! When she got home, she decided, she would write a piece about this for the school paper.

"Who's this one?" Robin asked. "He looks like my Uncle Joe."

Miss Tilly laughed. "Let's hope it stops at looks. That's Crippen, the wife killer. But if you want someone more up to date, there's Christie a little farther on. The police found a whole closet full of dead women in his kitchen. I suppose he—"

She stopped as steps sounded behind them. Voices rose excitedly. "Miss Tilly! Miss Tilly— it's *us*!"

Wheeling around, Robin saw three girls, the

eldest about seventeen and the youngest about twelve. They rushed at Miss Tilly, all talking at once, and the youngest hugged her. "Miss Tilly, we *do* miss you so! No one's such fun to go out with!"

Miss Tilly beamed at them. "Why, girls!" she said. "How lovely to see you again." She turned to Robin. "Robin, these are the White girls. I used to take them around a lot, but now Flora is seventeen, quite able to look after them." She smiled. "Girls, this is Robin Miller, from America."

The three girls shook hands with Robin. "You're in luck to have Miss Tilly," the eldest one said. "She's a super guide! No dull stuff."

They were being polite, Robin thought, but what they really wanted was to talk to Miss Tilly. "Look," Robin said, touching Miss Tilly's arm. "I'll walk on a little, slowly. You stay and talk with your friends."

Miss Tilly hesitated. "Well, just for a few minutes," she said. "You're not likely to be overcome with fright?"

Robin laughed, moving off. She saw figures of imprisoned lords, policemen who had turned crooks, killers like Lee Harvey Oswald. Not all of them seemed to have done really terrible things. Denis Collins, as a card near him said, had thrown a stone at King William IV—but the king was saved by the brim of his hat.

She stood for a long time before a group that puzzled her. It showed a pale, bald man kneeling beside a handsome hangman. The hangman was looking at a looped rope which hung from the ceiling. The card said: Peter Long, gardener at Greystone Hall, who killed the eighth lord of Greystone by scaring his horse and causing him to fall.

Understandable enough. But what was that other figure doing in the background? A tall, thin figure with a scarf covering the face.

Robin read the card again but it told her nothing about the figure in the background.

Glancing around, she saw that no one was near her. She had left Miss Tilly and the girls somewhere behind, around a corner and out of sight. Mark, though, might arrive at any minute.

Robin smiled to herself and ducked under the velvet rope that kept visitors from coming too close to the wax figures. If she pulled the scarf away from the face—a little tug would do it—she would be able to see what he looked like. Of course she would put the scarf back carefully.

The figure was very tall. She had to stand on her toes to reach the face. She stretched out her hand and her fingers touched the scarf.

Suddenly a hand shot out and grabbed her arm. "Hands off, little lady," a voice said. "I don't want to be rough with you!"

The voice was almost lost in the scarf. Robin gasped, and looked up. This was no wax figure! It was a living, breathing young *man*.

7

Robin tried to pull away but the young man held her fast. "Let go of me!" she cried. "I only wanted to look at your face. I thought you were a wax figure.

"So do many people when I make my visits," the voice said. "Some day I will teach them a lesson. They should save their interest for Peter Long, murderer of the eighth lord of Greystone."

Robin tried again to pull away but it was useless. She tripped, falling to her knees. "Poor little lady," the man said. "I will help you up and we will go somewhere to talk."

He was dragging her toward the heavy red curtains that formed the background of the group of figures. Robin screamed, and screamed again. The hand let go of her then, so suddenly that Robin fell again.

"Miss Tilly! Miss Tilly!" she cried, getting to

her feet and ducking back under the velvet rope. "Anyone—help!"

There was a sound of footsteps running. She stood there, shaking, as Miss Tilly rounded the corner, followed by the White girls. At sight of them, Robin pulled herself together.

"Robin, dear!" Miss Tilly ran to her. "Whatever is the matter?"

Robin managed a smile. "I'm okay," she said shakily. "But I had a fright. I ducked under the rope just now to look at a figure—and it was alive—a young man! He grabbed me by the arm—"

The White girls stared at her. "But there's no man here," the youngest one said. She started to duck under the rope but her sister stopped her.

"Stay back, Rose," Flora said. "You know you're not supposed to go near the figures." She looked at Robin curiously. "Are you *sure* there was a man? I mean—well, it's so easy to imagine things down here!"

"I was not imagining," Robin said crossly. "I'm—" She stopped as Mark came hurrying up.

"I just got off the lift and I heard someone yell," Mark said. "Was it you, Robin? What happened?"

"Robin thought one of the wax figures came to life!" Flora White said, as Robin hesitated. "Imagination, I'm sure. It's spooky down here, especially on your first visit."

"I was *not* imagining," Robin said again. Thinking it best to change the subject, she smiled at Flora. "Do you and Mark know each other?"

"Oh, yes! We're all from the same village. Greystone," Flora said. "This group of figures shows the man who murdered the eighth lord of Greystone, by the way."

"I know," Robin said shortly. She was watching Mark. He jumped over the velvet rope, went to the heavy red curtains, and pulled them back.

"Mark—Mark!" Miss Tilly started after him.

48

"Come back, dear boy. You're not supposed to go in there!"

There was no answer from Mark. But in a moment he was back again, shaking his head. "There's no one there, Robin," he said. "It's only an empty space with a few empty boxes." He grinned at her. "I guess maybe Flora's right." Then he asked, frowning, "Did Miss Tilly see him?"

Miss Tilly looked upset. "I was out of sight, round the corner talking to the girls. Robin walked on by herself."

Mark nodded. "So she was here alone. No wonder she imagined things. This is a spooky place even when it's full of visitors."

Inwardly, Robin groaned. But she wasn't going to argue with Mark. She'd just let it go.

"I daresay Robin could do with a nice cup of tea," Flora White said in a motherly way. "The teas aren't at all bad here."

Miss Tilly beamed. "Now *that's* a good idea! Will you girls join us? And Mark, of course."

The girls were sorry but had to refuse.

49

"We've a bus to catch," Flora said. "I do hope you have a good time in England, Robin."

After the girls left, Robin and Miss Tilly and Mark took the lift to the tearoom. After the Chamber of Horrors, it seemed warm and welcoming. There were pink-shaded lamps on the tables and there was a delicious smell of toast and apple pie.

Robin settled herself in a cane chair. "Let's have a huge tea," she said happily. "Getting a fright seems to make me hungry!"

"I haven't that excuse," Mark said. But he ate as much as Robin. Suddenly he said, "I'm really sorry to tell you this, Robin, but I'm afraid this is a goodbye party. I'm leaving for home tomorrow."

"Home?" Robin looked at him blankly. "I thought you were staying with your uncle for the summer?"

"Only part of it. I live in Greystone most of the year, as Flora said—my father is Vicar of Greystone Church." He turned suddenly to Miss Tilly.

"Why don't you bring Robin down for a tour of the Hall?" He smiled at Robin. "I know you take a dim view of history, but you really ought to see one of England's stately homes."

Robin's spirits rose. So there was going to be another meeting!

But Miss Tilly wasn't sure. "I sort of promised Robin no history," she said. "She's very much a twentieth-century girl. Mark's right, though, Robin. You really should see one of our stately homes."

"The present Greystone Hall's only a few centuries old," Mark said. "Built in 1781—carrying out the ideas of the sixth Lord Greystone. It's something to see, a huge place."

Robin pictured a vast building with room after room of curios. "I suppose it's a sort of museum," she said. "I don't like museums very much. They're so *dead*. Except the Fire Museum in New York City. That's full of the funniest old fire engines."

Mark laughed. "I don't think Greystone Hall is anything like a fire museum. But it certainly isn't dead. The rooms are all furnished—and the family lives in one wing. The rest of the Hall is open to visitors so there's plenty of life there. People come by the busload from all over England." He added, "But don't take a guided tour when you come. I know the Hall inside out and I can show you all the best parts."

8

They got back to the hotel about six and Mark went off to have dinner with his uncle. Robin herself had a late dinner with her aunt. They went to a part of the city with narrow streets and little Italian and French eating places crowded together.

In spite of her big tea, Robin was hungry. Not so Aunt Val. She pecked at her food, looking nervous. "How are you getting on with Miss Tilly?" she asked suddenly. "Such a funny little woman! Would you like me to ask them to send someone else?" Without waiting for an answer, she hurried on. "Robin, I'm so sorry but this trip isn't turning out at all as I expected. I will be free tomorrow, but after that I'm going to be tied up for a week or more. I have to go to three important sales, two in Scotland and one in Wales."

Robin smiled at her. "Relax," she said kindly. "And don't even dream about changing Miss

Tilly. She's fun, and she knows her stuff. One of these days I'm going to fix her hair for her— and get rid of that *hat*."

Aunt Val laughed. "That should help." She took a folder out of her bag. "I thought we could go to Hampton Court tomorrow, you and I. After that you can make your own plans. You don't have to stay in the city as long as you have Miss Tilly, you know. There are lots of places you can go by bus. Just let me know when you run out of money."

Aunt Val wanted to hear about Robin's visit to Madame Tussaud's, so Robin told her. She made the wax figures seem so real that Aunt Val shivered. Of course I can't tell her I was grabbed by that man, Robin thought. She'd never let me go anywhere without her again, not even with a dozen Miss Tillys.

On her way up to bed, Robin saw Mark, but he was busy showing visitors to their rooms. She walked close enough to him to say, "Miss Tilly and I will go to Greystone Hall the day after tomorrow."

"Oh, good!" Mark said. "Take the ten o'clock bus, and I'll be waiting for you in the old stable yard where the buses park."

"See you then," Robin said, giving him her nicest smile to make sure that he would remember her.

The next day, Robin and Aunt Val went to Hampton Court. What a great palace, Robin thought, but a bit tame after Madame Tussaud's. Maybe if she had known more about English history she would have got more out of it. As it was, she mixed up all those English kings.

It was more fun to be with Miss Tilly, Robin decided. Aunt Val had a thing about dates; she loved them. Miss Tilly didn't bother you with them, and when she told you anything, she told it in a funny way, all her own.

Next day, on the bus ride, Miss Tilly gave Robin a lot of facts about Greystone Hall. All interesting, with not too many dates. "The sixth lord, who built the place, was very, very rich," Miss Tilly said. "But it is hard for the present

55

lord and his family. It costs a fortune to keep up these houses, with all the grounds. So they have to open Greystone Hall to visitors. They even have pony rides for the children and serve teas."

"Let's have tea there, then," Robin said. "I'd like to have a lord waiting on me."

Miss Tilly was shocked. "Oh, no, the family keeps to its private wing. Though you do see them in the grounds sometimes. Two little boys, very fair and handsome." She sighed. "There are so many of these beautiful old halls in England, and so few of the owners have the money to keep them up."

"Where does Mark live?" Robin wanted to know.

"Oh, Mark. I told you his father was vicar of the parish church, didn't I? Such a lovely old church. Mark grew up in the village and knows the Hall well. He used to work in the gardens sometimes."

The bus reached a part of the country that was all narrow lanes. So narrow that Robin wondered what they would do if they met a flock of sheep. Cows would be even worse. She supposed, though, that animals would be kept safely in their fields. Such funny little fields, each with its high hedges and white, barred gate.

Suddenly Miss Tilly gave a squeak. "Look through the trees there, Robin. You can see the roof of Mark's home."

"Shall we get off the bus and surprise him?" Robin asked. But Miss Tilly looked so startled that she laughed and added quickly, "I'm only kidding." After all, she didn't want Miss Tilly to think she was boy crazy. Even if she was—a little.

"I don't think the bus would stop here," Miss Tilly said. "And anyway, Mark said he'd meet us in the stable yard. We'll be there in a few minutes."

The bus soon turned through tall iron gates and rolled up a drive edged with fine old trees. It came to a halt in front of a stable where four buses were unloading their passengers.

"We're at the back of the Hall. There's quite a crowd today," Miss Tilly said. "I don't see Mark anywhere, do you?"

"Maybe he's a bit late," Robin said. She stood there, looking around. But she had a strange feeling that Mark was not going to show up.

9

They waited for fifteen minutes, but Mark did not appear. "Something must have kept him. Mark is a dependable boy," Miss Tilly said. "Perhaps we had better join the guided tour?"

"That's okay with me," Robin said. It wasn't, though. She had looked forward to being shown around Greystone Hall by Mark.

"The tour starts at the front," Miss Tilly said. "The family uses a side door in the west wing."

They walked along by the side of the house, still keeping an eye out for Mark. When they rounded the corner, Robin gave a cry of delight. A wide terrace ran along the front of Greystone Hall. Lawns swept down to a wood, and there were fountains dancing in the sunlight.

She looked up at the Hall. What a huge place, she thought. Not quite as large as Hampton Court, but getting there. She wondered what it would be like to live in so large a home. Why, you could get lost on your way to bed!

The Hall was built of grey stone, on simple, classic lines with many tall windows that gleamed in the sunlight. A tour was gathering outside the main entrance door. "Please line up in orderly fashion, ladies and gentlemen," the guide called. "We'll start our tour with the Great Hall."

Robin gave a last look for Mark. "Let's stay right at the back," she said to Miss Tilly. "Then Mark will see us—if he comes."

Miss Tilly seemed to have forgotten Mark. She was pink with pleasure, eager to follow the tour. "Do take a little look at the paintings, Robin," she said. "There are some famous painters here—Reni and Lawrence and Mary Beale. My own favorite is *The Adoration of the Shepherds.* I could gaze at it for hours!" She looked around the entrance hall. "It used to hang here, but they must have moved it."

"I'll let you know if I spot it," Robin said, as they followed the other visitors into the first room. How could you ever relax in a room so

60

crowded with stuff? So much furniture—and none of it comfortable looking. Skinny gold chairs, and tables with curved legs and marble tops. And screens and statues and china vases.

As in Madame Tussaud's, red velvet ropes kept visitors from getting too close. Two by two, the men and women followed the guide. Like animals going into the ark, Robin thought.

Suddenly she saw Miss Tilly's favorite painting in a darkish corner of the second room they passed through. She pulled Miss Tilly's arm. "Drop out," she said. "I think I saw your painting back there."

Miss Tilly wheeled round and went back. "Why, yes, they've moved it. But I can scarcely see it from here!"

"Duck under the rope," Robin said. When Miss Tilly looked startled, she added, "I'll keep watch. Though they couldn't throw you into jail just for wanting a close-up of a painting."

"I'm not so sure," Miss Tilly said darkly. "There's been a lot of stealing from these old houses." Looking left and right, she ducked

61

under the rope and crossed the room to the picture.

After a few minutes, Robin went to the doorway and looked down the long hall. The guide and his party were disappearing around a corner. Part way down the hall, she saw a door with a sign saying PRIVATE. It must lead to the family quarters, Robin thought. Rooms that were alive, not cold and stuffed with history.

Moving toward the door, she noticed that it was open a few inches. As she wondered whether to poke her head around it, a little dog came running down the hall. He stopped at the private door, pawing it, trying to get in. It was too heavy for him to move, and he began to yap.

"Okay, dog, I'll open it." Robin pushed the door open and the dog ran in, wagging his tail.

She stood in the doorway and looked in. Another long passage, dimly lit. No paintings here, but what looked like a lot of photographs hanging on the walls.

Family pictures, Robin thought. She would

just take a quick look. She moved into the passage, leaving the door a little open so that she could make a fast get-away if anybody came.

The photographs were so amusing that she lost her sense of time. Some were yellow with age. Pictures of ladies in long dresses, playing some kind of game on the lawn. Pictures of children in sailor suits and buttoned boots.

Suddenly she heard footsteps and wheeled around. Two boys, about eight and ten, were coming down the passage. Very English looking, Robin thought, with that near-white hair and red-apple cheeks.

"I say, who are *you*?" the elder boy called. "You're not one of Mummy's guests, are you?"

They came up and stood staring at her, unsmiling.

"She came with one of the tours, silly," the younger boy said. "I bet she's an American. All Americans have red mouths and stuff on their eyelids."

"Except the men and boys," Robin said. But

neither of them smiled. She held out her hand to the elder boy. "But yes, I *am* American. My name's Robin Miller."

The boy shook hands politely. "I'm the Honorable Nigel, and he's the Honorable Bruce," he said. "Better not shake hands with him, Miss Miller. He is always sticky from worms and things."

Robin shook hands anyway. "How come you're called 'the Honorable'?"

The elder boy looked at her as if she were a halfwit. "Well, I'm the elder son of Lord Greystone. That's Daddy. Bruce is only the younger son, but he is called Honorable, too."

The Honorable Bruce gave Robin an unfriendly look. "Why did you come through that door?" he asked. "It says 'private.' Can't you read?"

"Of course she can read," Nigel said. "And since she *can* read, it is rather rude of her to come into the private part of the Hall."

"A little dog was caught on the other side of

the door," Robin said, wishing they would smile. "I opened it wide to let him in. Then— well, I suppose I *was* a bit rude but I wanted to take a look at those pictures."

The boys thought a minute. "Well, I don't suppose we need report you," Nigel said. He gave his brother a quick look. "If you'll follow us, we'll show you where you can join up with the tour."

Robin followed them, half annoyed, half amused. Down some stone stairs to a lower level, which was very dimly lit. No one seemed to be about down here and Robin wondered where the passage led. To coal cellars, maybe. Or wine cellars?

They stopped before an iron-studded door. Nigel pushed it open. "In there, please," he said.

Robin hung back. "But it's pitch dark! And I don't know the way. You had better go first."

"No, *you*," Bruce said. Both boys smiled at last. And Robin felt herself pushed sharply. She

stumbled forward into the darkness.

Behind her, she heard a dull noise as the door closed. Then, faintly, the sound of laughter, and of footsteps running away along the passage.

10

Robin turned to the door and felt for the knob. There was none. Her fingers moved to the keyhole. There was no key in it. Stooping, she looked through the keyhole but could see only a tiny part of the dimly lit passage.

"Dopes," she said out loud. "I suppose this is their idea of a joke." They would be back in a few minutes, she thought. But meantime it wasn't funny. Poor Miss Tilly would be looking for her—and Miss Tilly would never dream of going through a door marked PRIVATE.

Sooner or later, someone would come along the passage. Robin tried yelling through the keyhole and banging on the door. No use. Peering around in the darkness, she saw a window, set high up. But it was so small and dirty that almost no light came through it.

Maybe there was another door, with a knob or a key? Robin began to grope her way around the walls. They seemed to be paneled, but there was no second door. And the room was empty, unless there was a table or something in the middle of it.

Getting back to the door, she tried yelling and banging again. Nobody came. She sat down on the floor. She would have to wait until those boys chose to come back and let her out.

It was a long wait. Creepy, too, in the darkness. Robin began to be hungry. After a while she closed her eyes—and promptly fell asleep. Daddy always laughed about the way she fell asleep so easily. "One day we'll find her fast asleep in the supermarket with her head on the cabbages," he said once.

She woke with no idea of how long she had slept. Hours, probably. There was no light from the window now. It must be late. Or perhaps the day had turned dark.

She began to feel scared—and madder than ever at the boys. What had happened to them? Did they mean to leave her here? Did anyone ever come along that passage?

She told herself that someone would come looking for her sooner or later. Miss Tilly would have raised the alarm long ago. People would be hunting for her.

But not in the private part of the Hall. Not yet. They would more likely be searching the grounds. She wondered if Miss Tilly would come across Mark anywhere. He knew this place. He might be smart enough to find her.

Suddenly she froze. She could feel the little hairs standing up on the back of her neck. There was someone in the room with her! She could hear breathing. A cold hand touched hers, and Robin screamed. The hand moved away, and she got to her feet.

"Who's there? Who *are* you?" she cried. "Is it Nigel?—or Bruce?"

There was no answer. Only a little laugh. Soft, whispery, somehow frightening.

"Who *are* you?" Robin cried again.

Again there was no answer but the whispery laugh. It was moving away from her, to the other end of the room.

70

Robin began to hammer on the door. Hammer and scream. "Let me out, someone! Help! Let me out of here!"

Suddenly a key turned in the lock. The door was pushed open. A woman with a flashlight moved it around in the darkness. Robin brushed past her into the passage—and into Miss Tilly's arms.

Miss Tilly hugged her. "Oh, Robin, whatever happened to you?" she cried. "We've been looking for hours—" She stopped as the woman with the flashlight came out of the room. "Robin, this is Lady Greystone—she has been so worried about you!"

Robin gave Lady Greystone a quick look. "There's something in that room," she said. "It touched me—and I heard a strange laugh!"

"Something in the *room*!" Lady Greystone turned quickly, "Parker—Wilkins. Take this flashlight and search that room properly." She gave the torch to two men who were standing in the passage.

The men were back in a minute. "There is no

one in the room, your ladyship," one of them said. "We'll take a look down the passage and in the wine cellar."

"Yes, do!" But Lady Greystone was puzzled. "Nobody came out of the room, Parker! We would have seen them!"

"That's right, your ladyship." The men started off. "No harm in taking a look, though."

"How did you ever get down here?" Lady Greystone asked Robin. "Miss Tilly was sure you wouldn't go into the private part of the house. So we've been searching the grounds."

Robin told her about the little dog she had let through the door. "I just came a little bit into the passage, to look at the pictures," she said. "And I met the Honorable Nigel and the Honorable Bruce." Her anger at the boys returned, and her voice was sharp. "I don't think they were very honorable, though! They told me they'd show me where I could catch up with the tour. Instead, they pushed me into that room"—she shivered—"and went off with the key!"

Lady Greystone looked very upset. *"Nigel and Bruce?"* she said. "I don't understand! The key was on the floor outside the door. I suppose it was some kind of joke—but why didn't they come back and let you out?"

"Maybe they have poor memories," Robin said. "They didn't seem to like Americans, anyway. Maybe they—" She stopped as Lady Greystone gave a little cry.

"The ponies!" she cried. "Their new ponies! They came at lunchtime, and I told the boys they could go riding in the woods for the afternoon. They were so excited they must have forgotten all about you!"

Before Robin could say anything, Parker and Wilkins came back. "No one around, your ladyship." Parker smiled at Robin. "Maybe the young lady took a nap in there and had a bad dream?"

Robin went red. "I *did* take a nap, but it was no dream! It was real," she said crossly. Why did people always think she was dreaming—or imagining things?

73

"You had a very nasty fright," Lady Grey-stone said. "And I can't tell you how sorry I am! The boys will certainly hear from their father when he gets back." She looked at Miss Tilly. "Now, won't you both come upstairs and have some tea? Robin must be hungry after all this."

She *was* hungry, Robin thought, but she didn't want to have tea with Lady Greystone. She didn't want to see those boys again. All she wanted was to go back to the hotel and Aunt Val.

Miss Tilly looked at her watch. "I'm afraid we'll have to leave, your ladyship," she said. "It's almost time for the last bus. We can just make it if we hurry."

Lady Greystone still looked upset. "Very well," she said. "But before you go, please tell me where you are staying—and the name of your aunt. I must certainly call to say I'm sorry. And you will hear from my sons."

Robin said goodbye with a smile. She was able to smile now. In a few minutes she would be away from this place, safe again with Miss Tilly.

In the stable yard, the last visitors were piling into the bus. Robin and Miss Tilly got in, and Lady Greystone stood beside the bus to wave them away.

They were rolling down the tree-lined avenue when Robin started. "Look, Miss Tilly," she cried. "Isn't that Mark?"

A boy on a bicycle was riding quickly up the drive. Miss Tilly needed only a moment. "Yes, that's Mark," she said. "I expect he's going to the Hall to look for us."

"Too bad," Robin said. "He's only five or six hours late." She slid down in her seat, disgusted with her day at Greystone Hall.

11

That night, after Aunt Val had treated the very hungry Robin and Miss Tilly to a good dinner, Robin decided to go to bed early. She was getting undressed when Aunt Val came to her room. "There's a call for you, Robin. That nice boy, Mark Roper."

"Mark? Oh, good!" Robin reached for her robe. There was no telephone in her room, so she went along to Aunt Val's.

"Hi, Robin," Mark said. "I'm sorry I missed you at the Hall. I want to explain why I didn't turn up to show you around."

"Explain away," Robin said, trying to sound cold. "Some day I'll tell you all about the delightful day I had in that delightful Hall."

"I know about it! Lady Greystone told me," Mark said. "And when next I see those boys there's going to be trouble. Meantime I want to tell you what happened to *me*. I got a call to go to my school and I had to catch an early bus. I didn't even have time to leave a message for you at the Hall.''

"I thought schools left you alone during holidays,'' Robin said. "Mine does, anyway.''

Mark laughed. "So does mine, usually. But they wanted to tell me I've been chosen as an exchange student—and guess what? I'm going to the United States, to the Pingry School in New Jersey!''

"New Jersey!'' Robin squeaked. She couldn't help it. "I live in the next state, Pennsylvania.'' He'll be able to come and visit us, she thought.

"I know. I've been looking at maps,'' Mark said. "I hope I'll be able to see you sometime. I won't know anyone else in America.''

"I'll have Mom invite you,'' Robin said. "But—well, aren't we going to see each other again before I leave England?''

"I hope so,'' Mark said. "That's really what I'm calling about. Couldn't you give the Hall one more try? The fact is, I want you to help me play sleuth.''

"Play what?''

"Sleuth. Private eye. Detective—a 'tec, as they say here. I'm onto a little mystery and I thought you might have some ideas."

The telephone operator broke in, and Mark groaned. "I'll have to hang up, Robin, I've no more change. But I'll call you tomorrow. You be thinking it over." There was a click, and he was gone.

When Robin told Aunt Val that Mark wanted her to visit Greystone Hall again, her aunt laughed. "He may talk you into it," she said. "But I'll quite understand it if you don't want to go back there. We could invite Mark to dinner in London, if you like?"

"I like," Robin said. Giving her aunt a kiss, she went back to her own room and was soon asleep.

The next morning, she and Aunt Val had a late breakfast. "My train doesn't leave until eleven, and I'll be back very late," Aunt Val said. "Why don't you and Miss Tilly go somewhere nice for supper and then take in a show?"

"Oh, don't worry about *us*," Robin said. "We

won't be as hungry as we were last night after my adventure. And maybe we can get hot dogs in the Tower of London."

"The Tower of London?" Aunt Val was surprised, but not very. She was used to Robin's changes of plan. "I thought you'd decided on a trip to Kew Gardens?"

"That was last night when I was still in a state of shock," Robin said. "Today flowers seem a bit tame. Miss Tilly wants to show me the Traitors' Gate, where they used to unload the prisoners from the river boats. And the block where poor little Lady Jane Gray had her head chopped off for no good reason."

Aunt Val frowned. "Well, wherever you go, don't get too far from Miss Tilly. Yesterday was really nasty for you. I think—"

She stopped as the waiter came to their table. "There's a call for you, Miss Miller," he said. "Mr. Roper said to take it in his office, if you wish. Save you going upstairs."

Some change of plan for Aunt Val, Robin thought, wondering whether to think of her figure or order more toast and pile it with gin-

79

ger jam. Ginger jam was one of the best eatables in England.

She was happily eating, figure or not, when Miss Tilly came into the dining room. Robin groaned softly. Another hat, even more crazy than the last one. Straw, with a crown of poppies that bobbed up and down as Miss Tilly walked.

Miss Tilly wasn't hungry. "Mother made me have bacon and eggs this morning," she said. "She thinks I'm still starved after yesterday." She let Robin pour her some coffee.

Robin told her about Mark's telephone call of the evening before, and Miss Tilly nodded wisely. "I was sure he'd get in touch with you," she said. "How good that he's going to have a year in America! I know his father was hoping things would turn out that way for him."

She was even more interested in the mystery that Mark had hinted at. "I do so love a mystery," she said. "Not that I've ever been mixed up in one. That would be too much to hope." She and Robin tried to guess what Mark's mystery would be about, but with no success.

Aunt Val was taking a long time at the telephone, Robin thought. Funny, because she hated long calls. She always poked fun when Robin was talking on the telephone to Bunny after having left her only a few minutes before. It was Aunt Val who had made Daddy let her have her own telephone. "But for heaven's sake limit her to local calls," she had warned.

When Aunt Val came back to the table a few minutes later, she was pink with excitement. "Oh, good morning, Miss Tilly. Has Robin looked after you properly?" she asked. Without waiting for a reply, she turned to Robin. "You'll never guess who that was on the telephone!"

"Daddy?" But Aunt Val wouldn't go all starry-eyed over Daddy.

"Try again—on this side of the ocean."

"The Prince of Wales," Robin said. Now wouldn't that be something!

Aunt Val shook her head. "But you're getting warmer."

"Lady Greystone?" Miss Tilly clapped her hand over her mouth. "Oh, dear, how awful of me. You wanted Robin to guess!"

81

12

Robin wasn't as surprised as Aunt Val expected. "I forgot to tell you she said she'd be in touch—to say how sorry she was. Is she still mad at the boys?"

"She certainly is," Aunt Val said. "They're not allowed to ride their new ponies for a week."

Robin felt sorry for them, but not very. "Maybe they'll think twice before locking people up in dark rooms."

"But that's not all," her aunt said, her eyes shining. "The wonderful thing is that she wants you to come and stay with them for a week or so! The boys want to show you that they're not really little monsters."

Robin stared at her aunt, unbelieving. "Stay in the Hall? Behind all those private doors? But I don't know those people! They're strangers." She shook her head. "I don't think I'd care about visiting with them."

Aunt Val's face fell. "Oh, Robin!" she said. She must have thought Robin would jump at the invitation. She looked at Miss Tilly. "What do *you* think Robin should do, Miss Tilly?"

Miss Tilly was excited too. "Oh, I think she should *go*," she said. "She didn't see anything of the Hall yesterday. In a week she could really see all the house and grounds."

"It wouldn't be any fun running around with those silly kids," Robin said.

"But you wouldn't have to!" Miss Tilly cried. "Mark Roper will be there—or had you forgotten?"

Robin started. Actually, she had forgotten Mark for a moment. "Why, so he will," she said, weakening. "And if those boys get in my hair, he can tell them to buzz off."

Aunt Val smiled. "Then shall I telephone Lady Greystone and tell her you'd be delighted?" she asked.

Robin sighed. I didn't say *delighted,* she thought. Grownups are always putting words in your mouth.

Suddenly she thought of something. "But Aunt Val, what about Miss Tilly?" Surely Aunt Val had engaged Miss Tilly for a week or longer.

Aunt Val smiled. "Miss Tilly is invited too. Lady Greystone thought you would like to have someone you know with you. She says she doesn't expect you to be bothered with the boys." She looked at Miss Tilly. "Can you be away from home overnight for a week, Miss Tilly?"

Miss Tilly could scarcely speak with excitement. "Oh, yes, yes I can!" she said. "I'll get someone to stay with Mother! She wouldn't want me to miss such a chance!"

So that was that. Robin smiled at her. It would be fun to have Miss Tilly along. "But what about you, Aunt Val?" she asked. "When you get back at night, there'll be no one for you to have dinner with."

Aunt Val laughed. "Don't be so sure! There are one or two nice people in London I can look up. Anyway, I may have to stay overnight when I go to Scotland. This way, I'll know you are all right." Suddenly she looked a little worried. "But Robin, I don't want to *push* you to Greystone Hall. And remember, you can come back any time you want. If you're—well, uncomfortable or anything."

"Like a fish out of water?" Robin said. "I won't be. Honorables and ladyships don't scare me, Aunt Val." She gave her aunt a hug. "I'll call you from the Hall every night before I go to bed."

Miss Tilly had the last word. "You'd better telephone Mark. Won't he be pleased when he hears?" she said. "We can help him with his— his—"

She didn't finish. Because Robin shot her a look that said, "Be careful what you say in front of Aunt Val!"

13

As things turned out, Robin and Miss Tilly did not go to the Tower of London that day. "Would you mind if we saved it—and went shopping?" Miss Tilly asked. "I simply must buy something nice to wear at the Hall."

"And you need a new hat," Robin said firmly. "I'm going to treat you." As Miss Tilly began to protest, Robin said, "Please! Daddy gave me a lot of money and I've hardly spent anything."

They found a little hat shop where Miss Tilly tried on hat after hat, with Robin making faces and shaking her head.

"Here, try this!" Robin said suddenly, picking up a little cap-type hat in a cheery shade of red. "It'll make you look like Peter Pan." She laughed. "No, don't put it on so straight. Tilt it a bit."

Miss Tilly looked at herself in surprise. "I don't look at all like me," she said, "but that's just as well. I've never liked my face."

"You have a *nice* face," Robin said indignantly. "And that hat gives you an air. A Greystone Hall air." So Miss Tilly, beaming, allowed the clerk to put the hat in a little box.

Later in the day, they took the underground railway to Ealing, the neighborhood where Miss Tilly lived with her mother. Robin looked amusedly at the tiny row houses, each with its front yard glowing with flowers, as if everyone was trying to out-do his neighbor.

Mrs. Tilly proved to be just like her daughter, only older. She welcomed them warmly. "What a lovely surprise!" she said. "Emma is having such fun with you, Robin. I hear all about your adventures. What's going to happen next?" Her grey eyes lit up.

"You'll never guess, Mother!" Miss Tilly said. At top speed, she began to tell the old lady about the invitation to Greystone Hall.

Mrs. Tilly was as excited as her daughter. "It's like a dream! Greystone Hall has always been Emma's favorite place," she said. "Of course she's been there many, many times, taking visitors. You know it is one of what we call England's 'stately homes.'"

While Miss Tilly was upstairs, looking over her clothes, as she told Robin, Robin chatted comfortably with Mrs. Tilly and made friends with the big yellow cat.

They had supper with Mrs. Tilly in the snug little kitchen. "I'm afraid there's only mushrooms on toast," Mrs. Tilly said, fussing happily. "And apple pie with cheese. But you'll make up for it at Greystone Hall."

"Do you think we'll get strange food?" Robin asked. "Caviar and—and frogs' legs?"

Mrs. Tilly shook her head. "That would be Russian and French. I think you'll get good, healthy food—like the roast beef of Old England!"

"With cabbage?" Robin laughed. "This is a great country for cabbage."

Robin and Miss Tilly tore themselves away from Mrs. Tilly at last and got back to London in time to see a movie. Then Robin went to bed and was asleep before Aunt Val returned.

Next morning, Robin and her aunt had breakfast together. Now that the time had come for Robin to leave for Greystone Hall, Aunt Val was jumpy. "I hope I'm doing the right thing," she said, "letting you go off like this. I suppose I really should have talked to your mother."

Robin laughed. "Mom'd *kill* me if I didn't go! She's a good Democrat but she's crazy about people with titles. She sat through a boring lecture last month, just because it was given by *Sir* Somebody. Can't you see her running around telling everyone 'My daughter's staying with Lady Greystone, of Greystone Hall!'"

Aunt Val smiled, "I guess you're right. She and your dad will get a real kick out of this."

Miss Tilly arrived then, and they waited near the entrance until a car glided up to the hotel. "What do you know? It's a Rolls-Royce," Robin whispered to Miss Tilly. "I've only seen them in antique car shows."

"It looks a little old, but not antique," Miss Tilly said, "and how beautifully shiny it is!"

A uniformed driver came up the steps. "Good morning, miss," he said to Robin. "Are you the young lady for Greystone Hall?"

"Yes, I'm Robin Miller." She gave him her friendly smile. "Our cases are back there."

She and Miss Tilly climbed into the back seat. "Oops," Robin said. "It's like sitting on Jello." She added, "We have a Volks and a terrible old station wagon at home. All the seats are lumpy." This will really be something to tell Daddy, she thought, taking note of the speaking tube and the silver vases with real flowers in them.

The car went much faster than the bus had done. As they reached Greystone Village, Robin kept her eye out for Mark, but there was no sign of him. Soon they turned in through the iron gates and up the drive to the side entrance to Greystone Hall.

Lady Greystone and the boys were waiting to welcome them. "It's so nice to have you, Robin," Lady Greystone said. "And I'm sorry my husband isn't here—he's in New Zealand, visiting his brother."

She pushed Nigel forward, and he shook hands with Robin. "We're sorry we forgot you in the basement room," he said, as if he had learned it by heart. "Honestly, we didn't mean to. It was the ponies—"

"We didn't know you'd be afraid of the dark," Bruce said. He marched along at Robin's side, as Lady Greystone led the way into a comfortable living room. "Was there really a ghost or something that touched you?"

The memory made Robin feel cold. "Well, *I* thought so," she said shortly. "But everyone thinks I had a bad dream, so maybe they're right."

Lady Greystone rang a bell near the fireplace. "When Mary comes, she'll show you to your rooms," she said. "We've put Miss Tilly next door to you."

Robin thanked her. "I know I call you 'Lady Greystone,'" she said, "but it's rather a mouthful to call the boys 'Honorable Nigel' and 'Honorable Bruce!'"

Lady Greystone laughed. "The boys are called Nigel and Bruce—and worse names when they don't behave!"

The maid, Mary, appeared then and led them along passages and up a staircase to the second floor. "You're in the Pink Room, Miss Robin," she said. "And Miss Tilly is next to you."

Robin stood in the doorway, staring around. "I've never seen such an all-over pink room!" she said. "Only rooms with *bits* of pink, like sheets. And I've never slept in a bed with a canopy!"

"I'm told this is much like the room Princess Margaret had when she was a little girl," Mary said, opening a window and letting in the flower-sweet air. She went off with Miss Tilly then, and Robin could hear Miss Tilly's little cries of pleasure.

In two minutes, Miss Tilly was back. "My room is blue," she said, "and ever so many famous people have slept in the bed! I can't believe it, Robin. Emma Tilly sleeping in Greystone Hall!"

"There's a writing desk with paper with the address on it," Robin said. "You can write to your mother and all your friends." And I'll write to every last person at home, she thought. I'd better make a list.

After they had freshened up, Mary came back and took them down to the dining room. A surprise was waiting for Robin. Mark Roper was there, talking to Lady Greystone.

"I thought you'd enjoy having Mark lunch with us," Lady Greystone said to Robin. "And he has plans for you for this afternoon."

14

"So we meet again," Mark said. "This time on my home ground. Lady Greystone is trusting me to take you around."

"And there'll be no more frights," Lady Greystone said. "There's really nothing to upset you here, Robin. Of course we have our ghosts—all of these old places have them—but they are old women, quite harmless. One of them spins in the north attic, and the other is heard in the garden at night, playing a flute."

"The wind, probably," Robin said. "But I hope not. I'd like to meet a ghost."

Lady Greystone laughed. "We must try to arrange something, then." She turned to Miss Tilly. "Meantime, as Mark is taking Robin off for the afternoon, you may like to come with me to the fair in the next village. I promised to look in on it."

Miss Tilly's eyes shone. "Oh, yes, thank you! It's years since I've been to a village fair. "Will there be a wishing well—and a fortune teller?"

Lady Greystone looked amused. "There will—but don't put too much faith in the fortune teller. She's Mrs. Wilson, our cook!"

Lunch passed pleasantly, though without caviar or frogs' legs. They ate tender little lamb chops, peas with mint, and grilled tomatoes. Plums and cream followed.

During the meal, Lady Greystone and the boys asked questions about life in the United States. "It's very silly that we've never been there!" Lady Greystone said. "We're always meaning to fly to New York and then, instead, we go skiing in Switzerland or fishing in Norway. But really we shouldn't be away from the Hall these days." She frowned suddenly, looking worried, and Robin wondered why.

When lunch was over, the boys went to ride their ponies and the Rolls-Royce carried away Lady Greystone and Miss Tilly. "Now we can get going," Mark said, leading Robin out of the Hall. "I want to show you the folly."

"The *folly*?" Robin said. "What's that?"

"Don't you *know*?" Mark answered his own question. "No, I suppose you wouldn't. I don't suppose you have follies in America."

"If you mean acting crazy, we certainly do," Robin told him. "For instance, some kids in my school are building a computer out of cola cans. They say they're going to program it to do everybody's homework."

"Bright idea," Mark said. "But the kind of folly I'm talking about is a building—a tower or something."

"Oh, historic stuff," Robin said.

"Yes—and no. Some of the follies in England are historic. But you'd like them. They're crazy. They're built because somebody fancied a Greek temple in his garden, or a phony lighthouse, or the lady of the house wanted a pillar on the lawn with a stone pudding on top of it."

Robin laughed. "That sounds crazy enough, even for me. Is there a folly in the grounds here?"

"A very old one. The second Lord Greystone had a little round tower built for his private hermit or holy man. He shut the hermit up in it and ordered him to pray for him."

They crossed the old stable yard and entered

the Japanese garden. Visitors were crowding along the white pebbled paths, shouting to each other. "Look at the pagoda, children!" "Oh, what a pretty little bridge!" "No, Bobby, that's *not* a lake you can wade in!"

"I'll show you the gardens some other time, when there aren't so many visitors," Mark said. "The Fernery is full of rare plants, and there's a beautiful Orangery." He took Robin through a clump of trees, and out into a clearing. "Here's the folly!"

It was a high, round tower, built of grey stone. There was a single window, high up, and a door so small that only a dwarf could walk in. "I suppose they didn't want the hermit to have too many callers," Mark said. "I wonder how he got in himself without cracking his head."

"Probably doubled up with prayer," Robin said quickly. She looked at the thick growth of weeds around the base of the tower. "That door looks as if it hadn't been opened for years."

"You're right, it hasn't. The folly used to be

part of the tour but the visitors did so much damage inside it that the family closed it up, to preserve it. As for the weeds, well, there really aren't enough gardeners to take care of all the grounds. They work mostly in the special gardens."

Mark sat down with his back to a tree trunk. "Here, sit down a minute, Robin," he said. "I want to tell you about my mystery."

"Oh, good." Robin slid down beside him. "What a pity Miss Tilly isn't here—she loves mysteries!"

"You can tell her later—but don't tell anyone else," Mark said. "I don't know what to make of it, but I'm sure I've seen lights in the folly at night several times. Once at Easter and twice since I came home. Yet no one can get in."

"*Lights* with nobody there!" Robin said. "Where were you when you saw them?"

"In the grounds," Mark said. "I often take a walk round the grounds before I go to bed."

Robin had been thinking. "You've probably seen some reflections," she said. This didn't seem much of a mystery after all, she thought.

"Reflections of *what*?" Mark said. "There's nothing around here that would reflect."

"Flying saucers," Robin said. "Or don't you have them in England?"

"Not that I know of. Let's rule out reflections. What I've seen seem to be lights moving around inside the tower. Someone carrying a lantern, perhaps."

"Did you look through the window in the folly the next morning?" Robin asked.

"I did. I took a ladder. But the window's so dirty I couldn't see much. I tried to get it open but it's hopelessly stuck."

Robin thought a minute. "Do you think I could see the folly from my bedroom window?" she asked. "I'm in the Pink Room, if you know where that is."

"Yes, I know where the Pink Room is—and you *should* be able to see the folly from there. But it's rather far away. You'd need field glasses. I could bring a pair over for you later."

"Fine! Then I can look at the folly tonight. Miss Tilly can, too. And if we *both* see lights, then we'll know you're not imagining anything." *The way everyone thinks* I *imagine things,* Robin thought.

Then she remembered something. "Mark, do you suppose Lady Greystone has seen those lights and is worrying about them? Did you hear her say, at lunch, that they ought not to leave the Hall right now?"

"There may be something worrying her," Mark said, "but I don't think it's the lights. I don't think she has seen them. If she had, she'd have got one of the gardeners to bust open the door and see what's what."

"Why don't *you* bust open the door? You're strong enough," Robin said.

Mark looked shocked. "*Me* bust open the door? But it's not my folly—or my business, for that matter. And it may be nothing. Just the same, I'd like to clear up this little mystery on my own."

"With my help," said Robin.

"Of course with your help," Mark answered, smiling.

15

That evening after dinner, Robin did her duty by playing card games with the boys for over an hour. Because it seemed to matter to them, she even let them beat her. Her mind was else-where—in the folly.

About nine, she excused herself. "I'll beat you both tomorrow," she said. "Right now, I think I'll go to bed—if you'll show me the way."

"*Bed*?" Nigel looked at her in surprise. "Bruce and I simply *hate* bed. We're glad there are plenty of places to hide in this house."

They showed her up to her room and said good night. Not bad kids, really, Robin thought. When they had gone, she tapped at Miss Tilly's door.

Miss Tilly was reading but she tossed the book aside.

"Too much love stuff," Miss Tilly said. "I thought it was going to be a mystery. It's called

Gloria's Secret, but the secret is only Gloria's silly love affair!"

Robin laughed. "Well, I've brought you a nice little mystery from Mark. I suppose you know the folly in the grounds?"

"Of course. Built by the second lord of Greystone. It used to be open to the public but they had to close it up."

"Mark's been seeing lights in it at night," Robin said. "He wants us to find out who's in there, and why."

"And how they get in?" Miss Tilly said wisely. "They'd need a ladder to reach that high window. And anyway, it would be too small for anyone but a child to get through."

"How about a secret passage?" Robin asked. "I've read books about old English houses and they always have a secret passage."

"Or two—or three," Miss Tilly said. "Some of these old places have a number of passages."

"But why?" Robin said. "Isn't one secret passage enough?"

"Oh, they needed more than one," Miss Tilly explained. "Some were used for smuggling. And back in Cromwell's time, when Catholics were not allowed to hold services, they used to bring a priest to the sick by a secret passage. Sometimes the master of the house would use a passage to escape when his enemies came looking for him."

"That could be a lot of passages," Robin said, discouraged.

But Miss Tilly was not in the least upset. "We'll simply have to find the one that leads to the folly," she said.

Robin smiled. "You make it sound so easy!" And the Hall is so big, she thought. Maybe Mark wouldn't find the passage until she was home again in America. That would be too bad.

"Is Mark quite sure he wasn't seeing reflections of some kind?" Miss Tilly wanted to know.

"He seems to be sure—but I suppose he could be wrong," Robin said. She stopped talking as Mary came into the room. "Mark Roper left these for you, Miss Robin," the girl said, holding out a pair of field glasses.

"Oh, thank you, Mary." Then, as Mary looked curious, Robin added, "I may go bird-watching tomorrow. There must be wonderful birds in these gardens." That's not exactly a lie, she thought, I only said *may*.

Mary drew the blue curtains and turned down Miss Tilly's bed before bidding them good night. As soon as she had gone, Robin jumped up and opened the curtains again. "There's still a little daylight—these English evenings are so long," she said. "You can just see the folly from here."

The field glasses were strong. They seemed to bring the folly right up under her nose. But there were no lights. Only grey walls and that one high window.

She handed the glasses to Miss Tilly who

105

peered through them eagerly. "No lights," she reported. Then she stiffened, "Yes—wait! There *is* a light. Look!"

Robin almost grabbed the glasses. Yes, there was a light, and it was moving about. "A flashlight," she said. "Or maybe someone with a lantern."

They took turns looking until the light disappeared for good. After that, Robin found her way downstairs to the library to say good night to Lady Greystone. "I can find my room now, I think," she said. "If I get lost, I'll shout for help!"

"Do that." Lady Greystone smiled. "Sleep well, dear."

When she got back to her room, Miss Tilly was waiting for her. "I've just thought of someone who would know about the passages," she said.

Robin started. "Not someone in the family? Mark told me not to say anything to anyone but you."

"No, she's not family. I was thinking of Nanny Wills. She used to know my mother when they were girls."

"But why would she know about the passages?"

"Because she's lived here all her life—and she's touching eighty," Miss Tilly said. "She used to be nurse to the present Lord Greystone. And to the boys when they were in the nursery. She married the head gardener, and Lord Greystone gave them a cottage on the grounds. Nanny would be sure to know about passages under the Hall."

"She sounds fine—if she hasn't lost her memory by now," Robin said. "Could we make some excuse and go and see her tomorrow?"

Miss Tilly smiled. "We won't need an excuse. Nanny's always happy to see me, and she likes talking about the Hall. But we can't go tomorrow, Robin. Lady Greystone told me that she's taking us all on a picnic. We'll have to make it the day after tomorrow." She looked at the

107

little clock by the bedside. "Robin, don't you want to telephone your aunt before you go to bed?"

Robin jumped up. "I nearly forgot! But Aunt Val goes to bed late—she'll still be up."

After Miss Tilly left, Robin sat for a few minutes on the edge of her bed, wondering how much to tell Aunt Val about Mark's mystery. Nothing at all, she decided. Aunt Val would only beg her not to get mixed up in it, and that would spoil everything!

16

At breakfast next morning nothing was said about a picnic. Lady Greystone made polite chatter, but Robin noticed that she looked worried and ate nothing but one small piece of toast.

"You run along now, boys," she said when Nigel and Bruce had finished eating. "I've asked Mark to take you for a cross-country ride. Try to be back by teatime." She turned to Robin, "I'm so sorry about this, Robin. As I told Miss Tilly, I meant to take us all on a picnic to Bury Woods. But something has come up and, with my husband away, I'll have to attend to it." She smiled faintly. "As a matter of fact, I have to talk with a detective."

A *detective.* Robin's eyes widened, and she shot a look at Miss Tilly. Could it be about the lights in the folly? But surely Lady Greystone wouldn't call in a *detective*—

Lady Greystone poured herself a cup of coffee. "I might as well tell you what's been happening, but please don't say anything to *anyone*."

"I won't," Robin promised.

"And I'll be as silent as the grave," said Miss Tilly.

Lady Greystone sighed. "It's all very upsetting," she said. "We've been having some robberies in the Hall. They began at Easter and there have been several others since then."

"The paintings?" Miss Tilly was horrified. "Have any of the paintings been stolen? That *would* be a loss!"

"No, not paintings. So far they've only taken rather small things. Small, but valuable. Things that can't be replaced." She sighed again. "A lovely old silver candlestick from the sixteenth century. Two priceless jeweled fans. Silver and gold boxes."

"Are they all taken from rooms that are open to the public?" Robin asked.

Lady Greystone nodded. She glanced at her watch and got up. "I'll tell you more about it later. Meantime I hope you two can find something fun to do. Would you like to visit the stables, perhaps?"

Robin shook her head. "Horses turn me off," she said. "I can't ride, and they look as big as elephants." She smiled at Lady Greystone. "Please don't worry about us! There's such a lot to see, and Miss Tilly knows all about the gardens." We can visit Nanny Wills, she thought. It's a wonderful chance.

Miss Tilly agreed with her. "It's only a short walk through the grounds," she said, as they made their way to the side door of the Hall. "We can be back in time for lunch."

On their way, they talked about the robberies. "Do you think they could have anything to do with those lights in the folly?" Robin asked.

Miss Tilly didn't think so. "The robber wouldn't hang around," she said. "He'd be off to London—on one of the tour buses, probably. Looking innocent!" She nodded wisely. "And he'd probably sell the stolen things there—to somebody called a *fence*."

Nanny Wills's cottage had a picture postcard

charm. A front yard bursting with flowers. Roses climbing around the door. A white cat dozing on the step.

But Nanny herself was not a bit what Robin expected. She had pictured someone plump and pillowy, with a sweet, lined face. But Nanny was thin and bony, with sharp black eyes and a pointed chin.

Although she looked surprised, she welcomed them warmly. "Emma, it's good to see you," she said, bending to kiss Miss Tilly. "Come into the front room and tell me all about your dear mother."

The front room was so stuffed with furniture that there was very little space for the visitors. Miss Tilly pushed Robin forward gently. "This is Robin Miller, Nanny. She's from America and she's staying at the Hall."

Nanny shook hands, her bright eyes taking in Robin's face. "I like Americans," she said. "We see a lot of them here in summer. And they're very keen on old places—some of them would like to carry away the Hall, stone by stone."

"Robin wants to know if the Hall has any secret passages," Miss Tilly said.

"Secret passages!" Nanny gave a crow of laughter. "Oh, yes, it has its share. One ends up in the Japanese garden, but it's been blocked up for years. And—let me think. Yes, there's one that comes out in the folly."

Robin exchanged a quick look with Miss Tilly. "Do you know where it *starts,* Nanny?" she asked eagerly.

Nanny thought a minute. "In a little room in the lower basement."

"Is it a room with paneled walls?"

Nanny nodded. "That it is. You push one of the panels in a certain spot, and it slides open. But you have to know which one." Nanny frowned. "Come to think of it, I don't remember hearing that that passage was ever blocked up. Perhaps they didn't bother with it—there are so many more important things to spend money on."

"Did you ever go down the passage yourself, Nanny?" Robin wanted to know.

Nanny shook her head. "Not me. But Miss

Stella—that's his lordship's sister—she went down the passage to the folly when she was fifteen. His lordship dared her. But she never went again. She said bats got into her hair!"

That was all Nanny had to say about the passage. "I'll put the kettle on and make us a nice cup of tea. Emma, you show the young lady my album," she ordered, taking a fat red album out of a drawer in the sideboard.

The album was filled with pictures of the kind Robin had already seen in the Hall. She looked politely as Miss Tilly turned the pages. But Miss Tilly didn't know who the people were or anything about them, so Robin soon lost interest.

She was thinking how excited Mark would be when she told him where the passage started. She could tell him at teatime when he brought the boys home.

Suddenly she had a strange feeling that someone was staring at her. She looked up quickly. The door was open a little, and a pair of eyes were gazing fixedly at her through the crack.

17

The eyes staring at Robin were not Nanny Wills's eyes. They were blue and glittering. Then Robin heard a laugh. Not at all like Mark's or Miss Tilly's, or her own. This laugh was low, whispery—a spooky sort of laugh.

Robin jumped up. "There's someone staring at me through the door!"

Miss Tilly was putting away the album. Surprised, she turned to look at Robin. "Someone *staring* at you, dear?"

"And laughing! Didn't you hear it?" Robin made for the door but Miss Tilly was ahead of her, pushing it wide open.

"There's no one here now," Miss Tilly said, "and I didn't hear any laugh." She looked upset. "Can you be—well, imagining things?"

"No, I'm not imagining *anything*," Robin said crossly. "And I have very good eyes and ears!" Why did people always think she was dreaming things up! Seeing people who were not there and hearing sounds that no one else heard.

115

She certainly *had* seen those eyes, and she *had* heard that whispery laugh.

Nanny Wills came in then with a loaded tray and Miss Tilly told her, "Robin thinks someone was looking at her through the crack in the door."

Nanny Wills's answer surprised both of them. "So she did—but there's no cause to be upset. It's only Georgie. He loves to peek, but if you catch him at it, he runs away. Slippery as an eel, Georgie is."

"But who *is* Georgie, Nanny? I don't seem to remember him," Miss Tilly said.

"My grandson." Nanny began to pour tea from a fat brown teapot. "He's a good lad but"—she tapped her forehead—"Georgie's always been strange, ever since he was a little lad. There's a long name for what's wrong with Georgie. Fantasy something. He gets ideas. Sometimes he thinks he's the Lord of Greystone." She smiled, but sadly. "They've always been good to him at the Hall, let him have the run of the place. He's harmless, Georgie is."

116

"Does he live with you?" Robin wanted to know.

"Most of the time. Sometimes he stays with his married sister in London. He's good at getting about."

Nanny changed the subject then. Robin was enjoying a piece of plum cake when she heard the laugh again. It came from outside. Jumping up, she ran to the open window and looked out, but there was no one in sight. So she came back to the table, feeling silly.

Nanny Wills laughed. "You won't catch Georgie, unless he wants you to," she said. "I remember once, up at the Hall—"

But Robin wasn't listening. I know where I heard Georgie's laugh before, she was thinking. Of course! It was Georgie in that dark room—and he touched my hand, and laughed. She could scarcely wait to tell Miss Tilly.

On their way out, a few minutes later, Robin noticed a small photograph on the floor. She picked it up and looked at it—an ugly young man with narrow eyes and oily hair. He did not

117

look as if he belonged to Greystone Hall. "Here, Nanny," she said. "This must have dropped out of the album."

Nanny glanced at it and made a face. "*That* doesn't belong in the album," she said. "It's Georgie's—he must have put it in the drawer." She frowned. "It's Tom Hill. He used to work in the grounds here. He's always making up to Georgie—he even comes to see him here sometimes. I don't like him. He plays up to Georgie's idea that he is the Lord of Greystone."

After they had said their goodbyes and left the cottage behind, Robin turned excitedly to Miss Tilly. "I know where I heard that laugh of Georgie's!" she said. "It was when the boys shut me up. You all thought I was imagining it—but I wasn't. It was *Georgie.*"

"Georgie?" Miss Tilly squeaked. "But how did he get out of that room? Nobody saw him!"

Robin was struck by a sudden thought. "Could he—could he have got away through the secret passage?"

"I don't see why not," Miss Tilly said. "Nanny Wills said they gave him the run of the Hall. He must know every corner."

"He could have found the right panel to push," Robin said slowly as they walked on. "And I've just thought of something else. Could it be Georgie who goes in the folly with a lantern?"

Miss Tilly was not sure about that. "It *could*, I suppose. But why ever would he want to? It can't be pleasant walking along the passage. Very cold and damp, I should think. And I don't imagine he'd like getting bats in his hair any more than Stella did. Of course his hair is short, so they wouldn't want to *nest* there."

Robin laughed. "Bats don't really get in people's hair, Daddy told me," she said. She thought for a while. "It seems to me there's only one thing for us to do. We'll have to keep following Georgie and see where he goes."

Miss Tilly didn't like the idea. "Following Georgie wouldn't be easy. Remember, Nanny said he's as slippery as an eel. And where would we find him to start with?"

"Oh, we'll find him somehow," Robin said easily. "All we have to do is ask everyone we meet if they've seen Georgie—and there are three of us to do it, remember."

18

Reaching the Hall, Robin and Miss Tilly found Lady Greystone deep in talk with a fat, grey-haired man.

Lady Greystone waved to them to join her. "This is Detective Lane," she said. "He's on the trail of our robbers! Detective Lane, this is Miss Robin Miller, a guest from America. And Miss Tilly, from London." She smiled. "You can cross them off your list of possibles."

Detective Lane smiled at them. "With four tours a day, and with who knows how many people, I'm going to have my hands full."

Robin had one of her bright ideas. "Couldn't we help you?" she asked eagerly. "Miss Tilly and Mark and I could pretend to be tour people and tag along with them. Then, if we saw anything out-of-the-way, we could let you know."

Detective Lane seemed amused. He looked at Lady Greystone.

"It's not really such a bad idea, is it?" she

said. "I'm sure Robin and Mark have very sharp eyes. Miss Tilly, too."

Detective Lane thought for a while. Then he nodded slowly. "It can't do any harm. Lord knows, I'll need all the help I can get." He looked at Robin, frowning. "But be very careful not to draw attention to yourselves—or to me!"

He turned to Lady Greystone again. "On my way in, I saw a rather strange-looking young man helping himself to some roses. He didn't seem to be with a tour."

"Helping himself to the roses?" Lady Greystone repeated. "Was he about nineteen—good looking, with red hair?"

Detective Lane nodded. "That's the one."

"Then it's Georgie." Lady Greystone smiled. "You'll see him popping up everywhere. He has lived on the grounds since he was a very small boy." She frowned. "Georgie acts strangely sometimes, but he is quite harmless."

"Acts strangely?" Detective Lane took out his notebook.

"He isn't quite sure who he is. He has—well,

fancies. They started when he was very young. Sometimes he thinks he is the ninth lord of Greystone and he walks around the grounds, keeping an eye on his property."

"I've heard of that sort of thing," Detective Lane said. "Can't anything be done for him?"

"Up to now, no. But my husband has met a doctor in New Zealand who has had a good deal of success with a new treatment. He may be able to do something for Georgie."

"Let's hope so. He's a nice-looking lad," Detective Lane said. "Now, if your ladyship will let me look around inside the Hall—"

There were guests for dinner that night but Robin begged off. "I'm not much good at grownup talk," she told Lady Greystone. "If you'll excuse me, I'll spend the evening with Mark."

"Just as you like, dear. What will you do with yourselves?"

"Just talk, I guess," Robin said. "I have a lot to tell him—about playing detective tomorrow and everything."

"Lawson is driving the boys to a movie as a

treat," Lady Greystone said. "Perhaps you and Mark would like to go, too?"

"Oh, thank you!" Robin's mind worked quickly. The boys could sit in the front with Lawson and she and Mark could sit in the back and talk without being overheard.

Everything worked out well. By six they were on their way. Nigel and Bruce were deep in noisy talk with Lawson. Robin, in the back, was able to tell Mark what had been happening.

When she came to her visit to Nanny Wills and the eyes that stared at her through the door, Mark laughed so loudly that the boys turned around, surprised. "I haven't seen Georgie since I got back from London," Mark said. "What did they tell you about him?"

"That he has fancies but he's harmless. He thinks he's the ninth lord." Robin hurried on, wanting to know whether Mark thought that Georgie was the visitor to the folly.

Like Miss Tilly, Mark did not think so. "What would he want to do there? There's nothing in the folly but some old furniture."

"You don't think he'd use it as a place to be alone in?"

Mark shook his head. "There are plenty of other places, nicer ones. Like the little summer house in the Japanese garden."

Mark's interest took fire when Robin told him that they were going to help the detective. "Now *that* was a bright idea of yours, Robin," he said. "It'll be something useful to do!"

He didn't see any point in following Georgie. "Sooner or later we'll find out who goes to the folly. Meantime, let's play along with the detective."

But Robin was not ready to give up on Georgie. "Well, you and Miss Tilly help the detective," she said. "And I'll follow Georgie!"

19

Next morning, Robin went first to see Miss Tilly and Mark take their places in the line of visitors. "Be sure not to draw attention to Detective Lane—or to yourselves!" she warned them.

She watched with a smile as they started off, hanging back at the end of the line. Miss Tilly carried a guide book to make her look like a visitor. Mark talked to his neighbor but his eyes darted this way and that.

When they made their way toward the dining hall, Robin started off to look for Georgie. He was not in the front garden, nor near the fountains, nor in the stable yard. She asked a gardener but he shook his head. "I haven't seen Georgie for a day or two, miss. You might try the Orangery. He likes sitting there."

But Georgie was not in the Orangery. Nor in the Japanese garden.

At lunchtime Miss Tilly and Mark joined

Robin. The cook had packed a picnic lunch for them, and they ate it under a tree near the folly.

"I don't know about you two but I've had no luck yet," Robin said. "Georgie doesn't seem to be anywhere in the grounds."

"Could he be up a tree?" Miss Tilly asked. "When I was young and wanted to get away from people, I always climbed a tree."

"Trees don't sound like Georgie," Mark said. "Not quite the thing for a lord of Greystone. He's more likely to be sitting in the Rolls-Royce."

They told Robin about their own morning. "A few false alarms," Mark said. "Miss Tilly saw a woman drop out of the line and go off by herself—but she was only looking for a ladies' room!"

"And there was a man taking a great interest in that picture I love so much," Miss Tilly said. "When I stared at him, he gave me a nasty look and hurried away. I shall tell Detective Lane about him. I made notes in my notebook."

It was not until the next afternoon that Robin

spotted Georgie. A tour was making its way through the Great Hall, and he seemed to be with it. But he suddenly turned back.

She crossed the hall quickly, her heart beating faster. There he was, outside the door marked PRIVATE, the one through which she had followed the little dog.

Georgie opened the door quickly, went through it, and closed it quietly behind him.

Robin waited for a minute or two to give him time to walk on down the passage. Then she opened the door and went through.

A loud laugh made her jump. Georgie had not walked on down the passage. He had waited behind the door. Now he stood there, looking at her.

"You've been following me," he said. "I know! I know everything you do."

"No, you don't!" Robin said. Her voice shook a little but she told herself she wasn't afraid, just excited. "I'm not following anyone. I—I was looking for Mark Roper."

"Mark's gone round with the tour," Georgie

said. "So silly of him. He must know the Hall by now." He drew himself up and looked coldly at Robin. "By the way, young lady, do you know who I am?"

"Of course," Robin said. It was important to please him, to keep on his right side. "You're the ninth lord of Greystone!"

And she dropped him the low curtsy she had learned as a little girl in dancing school.

She had done the right thing. Georgie smiled, delighted with her. "Now you may come with me," he said. He looked up and down the passage. "No one is about, and I have something to show you."

He started off, walking in lordly fashion, and Robin followed meekly. Her heart beat faster as they reached the stone steps that led down to the lower basement and the little dark room.

But she had no thought of turning back. In a few minutes, she was sure, she would know if Georgie used the secret passage.

Georgie made for the little dark room. Opening the door, he waved Robin in and shut it behind them. Then, taking a flashlight from his pocket, he shone it directly onto her face. He laughed, this time the low, whispery laugh that made Robin afraid.

"Yes, I am right," he said. "You are the one, as I thought. Your name is Robin. I have seen you before. Do you know where?"

"Yes, in Nanny Wills's cottage—your lordship," Robin said. She was glad that her voice sounded steady.

"Ah, Nanny. A good woman. But that's not what I mean. I saw you before that. Several days ago."

Robin shook her head. "I can't think *where* you saw me. I was in London then."

Georgie laughed again. "Have a good look at me," he said. He turned the flashlight so that it lit up his face. The gleaming blue eyes, the red hair falling over his forehead, the thin, smiling lips.

Robin shook her head again. "I'm sorry, your lordship, but I can't have seen you before. I would have remembered your face."

"Of course," Georgie said. "I remember now. I had a scarf over my face. But you saw me— you saw me in Madame Tussaud's!"

"Madame Tussaud's!" Robin cried. "Yes! You were standing at the back of the other figures."

Georgie nodded. "I like to go to Madame Tussaud's. I stand there and I wink. Or I yawn. And a silly visitor sees me and calls to his friends. But then I am as still as a wax figure again and his friends laugh at him."

He waited for Robin to say something admiring. So she said, "You must be very clever, your lordship. I remember now, I thought you were a wax figure too, until you moved and scared me."

"I wanted to make friends with you in Madame Tussaud's, but you were silly. You yelled and screamed, and I had to leave quickly." He put a hand on her arm, and Robin started. "But now I've found you again and I am going to share my secret with you."

20

Robin looked at him eagerly. "Do you mean the secret of how to open the panel, your lordship?"

Georgie shook his head. "The secret of the panel is simple." He walked across the little room and shone the flashlight on the second panel from the floor. "I keep it oiled," he said, turning to Robin. "This passage leads to my folly."

"I have seen your folly," Robin said, smiling. "But only from the outside."

"I do not allow people to go inside," Georgie said grandly. "But I like you, Robin. I want you to be my friend. So I will take you into the folly and show you my treasures."

Robin moved toward the panel. She was not afraid. Georgie liked her. He would take her to the folly, and perhaps he would tell her if he went there by night. She followed him down some rough stone steps.

As they started along the passage, Robin

stretched out her hands to find how wide it was. They hit cold stone. She raised her hand and touched the roof a few inches over her head. Georgie, she saw, had to stoop a little.

"Are there bats in here, your lordship?" she asked suddenly, remembering Stella's journey.

"Of course not. Bats live in caves," Georgie said. "There may be mice, or spiders. Are you afraid of mice?"

"No, I like them," Robin said. She tripped over a stone and Georgie turned quickly. "Mind how you walk, Robin," he said. "The path is rough in parts."

On they walked. Robin kept her hands on the stone walls to guide herself. Once there was a break in one of the walls. Another passage? Robin wondered. She could not tell how long they had been walking. Three minutes? Five? Then Georgie suddenly stood still and directed the beam of his flashlight upward. Robin saw a trapdoor, bolted.

Georgie slid back the bolt. "I keep it oiled, like the panel," he said. He pushed up the trapdoor.

"Now we are at my folly. Can you climb in?"

Robin swung herself up through the opening. She could see nothing but a window, high in the wall. A little daylight showed through it.

In a second, Georgie was beside her. He closed the trapdoor. "Stay still, Robin," he said. "I am going to light the lanterns."

He moved away from her and Robin heard him strike a match. He lit two lanterns and set one down on a bench. The other he carried with him. "Now come!" he said, his voice filled with pride. "I will show you my secret."

Taking Robin's hand, he pulled her with him, holding the lantern high with his other hand.

Robin saw a wooden table, very large, against the farther wall of the folly. She let out a cry. It was piled with silver boxes, clocks, pipe cases, figures of fine china, gold and silver candlesticks, fans, bells, and more. All looked rare and valuable.

"My treasures," Georgie said, setting down the lantern in the middle of the table. "Beautiful, aren't they?" He held up a golden candlestick. "This candle used to light my lady mother up to bed." He put it down gently. "And this is the fan she took to balls." He smiled at Robin, who was speechless. "If you are good, I will give you something for yourself."

Robin's head was spinning. She was about to pick up a bracelet made from gold coins when Georgie said quickly, "Don't touch! No one is allowed to touch my treasures!"

Robin drew back. "But your lordship," she said, "don't all these beautiful things belong in your Hall? Why have you brought them here?"

Georgie frowned. "I have been told that my Hall is no longer a safe place. At one time, only friends came to visit . . . and sometimes the King, to break his journey. But today strangers come and go all day. They try to touch things. My treasures are safer here."

The folly was chilly and Robin was getting cold, but she did not want to hurry him. She watched as he picked up the treasures, one by one, and showed them to her. "It will take weeks to bring everything here," Georgie said. "I come by night to clean and polish. I hide in the Hall until everyone has gone to bed. Then I come through the passage."

"Don't people see light shining from the folly?" Robin asked.

Georgie shook his head. "They are all in bed," he said simply.

"All this is very exciting, your lordship." Robin gave him her nicest smile. "You have been very kind, showing me your treasures. But we had better be going back now, don't you think?" As he began to shake his head, she added, "It must be nearly lunchtime. I'm getting very hungry."

Georgie frowned at her. "I'll bring you something to eat. I don't want you to leave yet. I like your company. I'll get food at the cottage. Or perhaps in the village. Or I may ask my cook to make us some stuffed eggs—"

He broke off at a sudden sound. The trap-door opened and a thin, dark young man climbed into the folly. "I've had a time getting here, your lordship," he told Georgie. "There's a fellow in the Hall who looks like a 'tec. He's keeping an eye on the visitors."

"A detective. I know," Georgie said. "That's why I did not take the painting."

"*What*?" The young man stared at Georgie, his face reddening. "You didn't get it? Why you—" He stopped as Robin moved out of the shadows and he saw her for the first time. "Who's this girl? And what is she doing here—your lordship?"

Georgie smiled. "Her name is Robin. She's my new friend. She is staying in the Hall and I'm showing her some of my treasures."

"Your lordship should be more careful," the young man said sharply. Listening to him, Robin decided that he was playing up to Georgie, just as she had herself. Pretending to believe that poor Georgie was really the Lord of Greystone. But he sounded as if he was very angry. Even in the dim light Robin could see the glint in his narrow, close-set eyes.

Suddenly she remembered where she had seen this young man before! He was Tom Hill, the man in the photograph she had picked up in Nanny Wills's cottage.

The man Nanny Wills didn't trust!

21

Robin looked quickly from one young man to the other. Georgie was smiling at Tom. "You can keep Robin company," he said. "She is hungry. I am going to the village for food."

Tom Hill's face was dark. For a few seconds he did not reply. Then he smiled back at Georgie. "I have a better idea, your lordship. I'll go through the stables and ask Nanny Wills to make us some sandwiches. While I'm gone, you can be getting the painting."

Georgie frowned. "But the detective—"

"You can give him the slip. He can't be everywhere at once. The servants know you and trust you." Tom grinned. An evil grin, Robin thought. "If anyone sees you, say you're taking the painting to be cleaned. You're smart enough to get away with it, your lordship."

Georgie nodded. "That is true."

The two men started for the trapdoor. Robin let out a cry. "Take me with you, your lordship!'' she begged. "I'll be afraid here, all alone in the folly!''

But Georgie had already jumped into the passage and did not hear her.

Tom Hill pushed her farther back into the room. "When I get back I'll deal with you, young lady. You know too much for my safety.''

Robin felt a chill of fear. "Please let me go!'' she begged. She put a hand on his arm. "I promise I won't tell anybody anything!''

Tom Hill shook her off. "I've never met a girl who can keep her mouth shut,'' he said. And he jumped lightly through the open trapdoor and let it slam behind him.

For a moment, Robin froze. Then she went to the trapdoor and tugged at the iron ring. It was no use. Tom Hill had slid the bolt over from below.

She sat down on the little bench at the table. She would have to think. She tried to tell herself that Tom Hill did not mean to harm her. But he was an evil man. She felt sure of that.

She began to walk around the folly. There

must be *some* way out, she thought. If only she could reach the high window. She could smash the pane with one of Georgie's candlesticks and yell for help. There were usually visitors walking in the gardens. Surely someone would hear her!

Her eyes lit on the little bench. If she pushed the table under the window and set the bench on it, she might just be able to reach the bottom pane.

She tried moving the table, but it was too heavy. Carefully, she unloaded Georgie's treasures and set them on the floor. Then she moved the table, inch by inch, until it was under the window. She lifted the little bench onto it and pushed it into place.

Next, she set a candlestick on the little bench. Then she climbed up. Good! Her head was almost level with the center of the bottom pane. The glass was dirty but she could see out fairly well.

As she bent to pick up the candlestick, she heard the bolt of the trapdoor slide over. Georgie, she thought. Please let it be Georgie!

But, looking down, she saw that it was Tom Hill. He shut the door and came quickly toward her, his eyes angry. "What do you think you're doing up there?" he shouted. "Come down before I drag you down."

As she climbed down, shaking, he watched her with narrowed eyes. "I don't like people who get in my way," he said. "I've got to get rid of you—but how?" He took a length of rope that had been wound around his waist under his jacket, and grinned. "I picked this up in the stables. I had an idea it would come in handy."

Pushing Robin down on the floor, he tied her arms behind her back, and then tied her ankles. Only pride kept Robin from crying out as the rope bit into her flesh.

He was turning away when the trapdoor opened and Georgie held up a small painting. "Tom, take it," he called.

As Tom set the painting down on the table, Georgie climbed into the room. He saw Robin on the floor and stared down at her, puzzled. "Why are you tied up, Robin?" he asked, stooping to help her.

"Don't free her, your lordship!" Tom shouted. "That girl was trying to steal your treasures! I just caught her in time!"

Georgie shook his head. "Not Robin," he said. "That is a silly story, Tom. Robin is my friend. And I'm going to untie her." He drew himself up. "You seem to forget that I am the Lord of Greystone and can do what I wish."

Tom grinned an ugly grin that disappeared as he unwound a second length of rope. Before Georgie could take in what was happening, he was tied up, too. Then Tom pulled Robin around so that she and Georgie were back to back. Robin was facing the high window and Georgie faced into the room.

"I'll be off now, Georgie-boy," Tom said, picking up the painting. He waved a mocking goodbye. "And thanks for making me rich at last. I've got a wealthy buyer for this painting.

But before I leave for good"—his voice made Robin feel even colder—"I promise you, I'll be back."

"You can't *do* this, Tom!" Georgie shouted after him. "You can't sell that painting. I promised it to you because you were my friend. You said you wanted to hang it in your room. But you're *not* my friend—and you can't have the picture."

He stopped, his jaw dropping. Because Tom had gone, taking the painting with him.

22

"Now what can we do?" Robin said. She shivered. "I don't trust Tom one inch." She twisted around to look at Georgie, who began to push himself toward the trapdoor with his feet. "Don't be afraid, Robin," he said. "I will get us out of here."

"But how can you lift the trapdoor with your hands tied behind you?" Robin wanted to know.

Georgie thought a minute. "I can't reach *my* hands but I can reach *yours*," he said. "I will untie the knots with my teeth. The lords of Greystone have very strong teeth."

"It's worth a try," Robin began—and broke off, staring up at the window. Someone was tapping and trying to look in. "It's Miss Tilly!" Robin yelled. "Georgie—your lordship—it's Miss Tilly! She must be on a ladder."

Georgie twisted around to look. "Who?" he asked."

"My friend," Robin said. "You must have seen her that day in Nanny Wills's cottage."

"Ah, yes. Through the door," Georgie said. "But how does she know we're here?"

"She must have guessed where I might be. She's a good guesser," Robin said. She did not want to hurt Georgie by telling him how she had tricked him into taking her to the folly. And how Miss Tilly and Mark knew all about it.

Miss Tilly's nose was pressed against the pane. "I wonder if she can see us," Robin said. "The window's so dirty." Then she smiled as Miss Tilly brushed the pane with her sleeve and peered through, waving. "Good! She spotted us. Trust Miss Tilly!"

After a minute or two, Miss Tilly disappeared. "I hope she'll bring help before Tom gets back," Robin said. Her voice shook a little.

"I thought he was my friend," Georgie said sadly. "I don't want him to sell my painting."

"Don't worry," Robin said. "We'll get it back." But she wondered how.

She and Georgie sat in silence for what felt

147

like a long time. Then both of them started as they heard a tapping sound. Was it Tom? Robin wondered. Oh, she hoped not. She hadn't yet thought of a way to escape from him.

She stared around the room. The noise seemed to be coming from the wall of the folly. For the first time, Robin realized that the inner walls were made of dark paneled wood. Low down, there was a very small door, fitted into the wall so tightly that it seemed to be part of the paneling.

"The tapping is coming from that little door!" Robin cried. "Do you see it, Georgie?"

"Yes, and someone is pushing it open!" Georgie said.

Inch by inch, the little door gave way. And suddenly Robin laughed aloud. Miss Tilly, on hands and knees, was crawling through the opening.

"Miss Tilly, you made it!" Robin cried. "Oh, Miss Tilly, you're wonderful."

Miss Tilly got to her feet, brushing at her

dress. "That was rather a tight fit," she said. "Wilkins pried the door open. But he and the detective are both too fat to get through that little space. They're waiting for us outside." She bent and started to undo the rope from Robin's ankles. "Who tied you up like this?"

"I'll tell you later. But now we'd better untie Georgie," Robin said. "He can go out to the men. You and I have to take Tom Hill prisoner."

"Tom Hill?" Miss Tilly said, puzzled. She began to untie Georgie. "Who's he?"

"Oh, *you* know. The man Nanny Wills doesn't trust. He tricked Georgie into giving him the Lawrence painting from the Hall. He just took it away. He is going to sell it and be rich." Her words came tumbling out. "Before he said he was going to the stables—maybe that's where he took the painting. There's another passage—" Her voice was unsteady. "But by now he may be on his way back to—well, get rid of *me*. He says I know too much."

"Get rid of *you*!" Miss Tilly was deeply shocked. "We can't have that!"

"I've got a plan to stop him," Robin cried. "Maybe you and I can catch him where the passages join."

She turned to Georgie. "Will your lordship please go and tell Wilkins and the detective to run to the stables? You go, too. If Tom Hill is still there, grab him! If not, he'll be in the passage and Miss Tilly and I will catch him and try to hold him till you come."

Georgie nodded. "Yes, yes. I see. But be careful, Robin." He began to crawl slowly through the little door.

Robin picked up a candlestick. "I'll use this to knock Tom out—and we'll take these ropes to tie him up—" She stopped as Miss Tilly shook her head.

"Here's all we need, Robin." She held up an old-fashioned string bag with two bananas in it. "The cook gave me this nice old bag. I brought bananas in case you were hungry." As Robin watched, puzzled, Miss Tilly took out the bananas and put them on the table. "*You* can trip Tom up, and I'll catch his head in this net—

150

like a fish! If he tries to get his head out, I'll pull the draw-strings tighter and he'll stop. He'll be afraid of choking!"

Robin laughed. She couldn't help it. "You're a wonder, Miss Tilly," she said. "It sounds crazy, but it may work."

"We'll make sure it does," Miss Tilly said. "But the passage will be dark, won't it? We'd better take one of those lanterns."

They climbed down through the trapdoor and walked to where the other passage branched off. Before they got there, Robin set the lantern on the ground. "Do you think Tom Hill will see any light from our lantern as he comes down the passage?" she asked Miss Tilly.

"No, dear, I don't." Miss Tilly took up her position on the far side of the opening. "The light doesn't reach far. It's almost dark here."

"Good," Robin said. She stood just before the opening, opposite Miss Tilly, ready to kick out her foot and bring Tom crashing down.

Miss Tilly, unafraid, hummed softly as they

151

waited. But Robin's heart beat fast. "Here he comes," she whispered suddenly. She had heard the sounds of hurrying footsteps.

As Tom started to round the corner into the long passage, Robin shot out her foot and tripped him up. He fell headlong, dropping his flashlight and letting out a cry of pain and surprise. Before he could get to his feet, Miss Tilly was sitting on his back, pulling the string bag over his head. "Got him!" she said happily. "Quick, Robin, sit on him with me. Our fish may be stronger than he looks!"

As Robin sat down on his back, Tom Hill struck out with his legs and arms. But Miss Tilly was ready. "None of that!" she told him, tightening the drawstrings of the bag around his neck. "Keep still, and stop trying to get up."

"Or you'll choke," Robin added sweetly. But she was not quite as cool as she sounded. She was hoping that Detective Lane and Wilkins would not be long.

"Here come the men. I see their light!" Miss

Tilly cried, bouncing up and down excitedly on Tom's back. "Look, Georgie's with them—and Mark, too!"

When the men reached them, Detective Lane wasted no words. He grabbed Tom and hauled him to his feet. Then he saw the string bag over Tom's angry face and laughed. "Whose idea was *that*?" he asked. "We'll keep him hooked in there for a while."

"Robin—Miss Tilly. Are you okay?" Mark asked, as Wilkins and Detective Lane started off along the passage with their prisoner. "I've been looking everywhere for you. Then I saw Georgie heading for the stables, and I followed to ask him if he had seen you."

"Robin is very brave," Georgie said. "Some day I will thank her properly." He frowned. "But now I—I'd better go." Before they could say anything, he turned and ran down the other passage.

23

Ten minutes later, back in the Hall, Robin told Lady Greystone all that had happened, beginning with her meeting with Georgie in Madame Tussaud's. When she stopped for breath, Miss Tilly or Mark helped out.

Lady Greystone kept shaking her head as if she couldn't take it all in. "I simply can't believe it!" she said. "Poor Georgie. But how good it is to know that nothing was really stolen." She laughed. "We'd better get those passages blocked up as soon as possible. When the boys find out about them, they'll start disappearing down there!" She got up. "I must call my husband! He'll be so glad to hear we haven't been robbed."

At the door she turned, smiling. "We'll tell the boys later—and we'll have a festive dinner for everyone tonight. Including Detective Lane."

Dinner that night was a wonderful meal, with

all the things Robin liked most to eat. Detective Lane, who had to hear the whole story, was highly amused. "You have the makings of a good detective," he told Robin. "And Miss Tilly, too." He made a funny face. "I was in charge of the case, but I don't feel I've done anything. You two have left me nothing to solve!"

He was wrong about that. As they were having dessert, a maid came in and whispered to Lady Greystone, who excused herself and left the room. When she came back, she looked upset.

"That was Nanny Wills," she said. "She found a note in a plant pot in her kitchen. From Georgie. He seemed very mixed-up about everything and said he was going away. But Nanny says he is not at his sister's house, in London."

Oh, poor Georgie, Robin thought. In all this excitement, no one had bothered about him. If he had run away, it would be *her* fault. He must be upset that everyone now knew about the treasures in his folly. The ninth lord of Greystone must think she had betrayed him! And on top of that, he had found out that Tom Hill was a false friend.

"He can't have got very far," Detective Lane said. "And with that red hair he won't be hard to trace."

"Perhaps he's hiding in Madame Tussaud's," Robin said eagerly. "We could go there to-morrow!"

Detective Lane held up his hand. "Not so fast, young lady. If Lady Greystone sees fit, you'd better leave Georgie to me." He smiled at Lady Greystone. "After all, I haven't earned my fee yet." He stood up. "If you'll excuse me, I'll start after him now."

Lady Greystone considered. "Yes, that would be best. And I'd like you to—well, keep an eye on Georgie until my husband gets home at the end of the month. Then we'll have to decide what to do about him in the future."

Robin was disappointed, but only for a moment. "You young people deserve to have some fun after all this," Lady Greystone said. "Robin won't have much longer in England. We'll have to take her to all the places she hasn't had a chance to see!"

24

Lady Greystone was as good as her word.
The next few days passed in a whirl of sight-
seeing. The Rolls-Royce took them to the
Tower of London, to Windsor Castle, to Kew
Gardens. Nigel and Bruce acted as guides.
"Don't trust them too far," Lady Greystone
warned. "They make up English history when
it suits them and they *never* remember dates!"

Aunt Val came early the day Robin was to
leave, and Lady Greystone herself showed her
around the Hall and the gardens.

Saying goodbye was sad. To her surprise
and theirs, Robin kissed the boys, who returned her kisses politely. "I've had a wonderful time," she told Lady Greystone. "I do hope
I can come back some day—and see all the
other follies in England."

Saying goodbye to Miss Tilly was the hard-
est, but Miss Tilly, as usual, was cheerful.
"You'll be back, Robin, I know," she said.

"Americans think nothing of hopping to and fro across the ocean!"

Robin and her aunt had one day together, shopping for gifts to take home. Aunt Val was tired. "But it's been a good business trip for me," she said. "As for you, I think you've had enough excitement to satisfy even *you*."

There was one more surprise for Robin. On the day of their departure, she and Aunt Val were at the Heathrow Terminal when they suddenly heard voices. "Robin! Robin—it's *us*!"

Robin could scarcely believe her eyes. There they were, all of them! Lady Greystone and the boys. Mark. And Miss Tilly in her little cap hat.

"We wanted to have one more look at you," Lady Greystone said. "And I wanted to tell you that we will certainly pay a visit to the United States next year. What's more, Miss Tilly will come along to keep an eye on the boys!"

"Oh, wonderful," Robin said. "But don't expect anything very exciting. Nothing ever happens where I live."

Mark laughed at that. "Don't be too sure,"

159

he told Lady Greystone. "Things have a way of happening when Robin is around."

Lady Greystone took a small package from her bag. "We decided that Robin ought to have one of the treasures of Greystone Hall," she said. "You can open it during your flight." She smiled. "I've written out its history for you, but you don't have to read it."

A treasure from Greystone Hall! "I'll keep it forever and show it to everyone!" Robin said, kissing Lady Greystone gratefully. Then she had to turn away because she felt tears coming.

On the flight home, she unpacked her treasure. It was a beautiful little silver clock, old and very delicate, in a soft leather carrying case.

When they neared the coast of America, Robin's spirits began to rise. It would be good to be home again, with Mom and Daddy. And *what* a tale she had to tell to Bunny and Eve!